THE DAUPHIN DECEPTION

An Alex Hunt Adventure Thriller

URCELIA TEIXEIRA

Independently Published
by
Urcelia Teixeira

To the group of die-hard Alex Hunt fans who started this adventure alongside Alex and me; you know who you are!

I will continue to help you escape the aches and pains, doctor's visits, cancer treatments, hardships, fights against addiction, loneliness, and tedious hours at work.

Thank you for sticking with us!

Onwards and Upwards!

Receive a FREE copy of the prequel and see where it all started!

NOT AVAILABLE ANYWHERE ELSE!

Click on image or enter http://download.urcelia.com in your browser

PREFACE

On June 8, 1795, Louis Charles Bourbon, mysteriously died in a small, dark room in Paris, France—or so it is believed.

As the only living son of King Louis XVI and Marie Antoinette, the young Louis Charles was destined to take the French throne.

But, on July 3, 1793, with the outbreak of the French Revolution and at only eight years old, the young prince was separated from his mother when she was sentenced to death by guillotine.

The Dauphin—the title given to the heir apparent to the throne of France — was locked up in a dark room in the Temple fortress where he was ill-treated and neglected for two years.

Legend has it that the boy fell ill and died of scrofula, putting an end to the monarchy for good.

His body was never seen nor found, and the truth behind his supposed death still holds mystery... until now!

PROLOGUE

SPRING, 1792 – THREE YEARS INTO CAPTIVITY

"Madame, did you hear?" her lady in waiting burst into her chambers. "They forced the King's hand to declare war on Austria," she continued.

Marie-Antoinette briefly looked up from the tapestry on her lap. Under any normal circumstances, the announcement would have been devastating. Instead, the news left the Queen elated.

"Madame, did you hear me?"

"Yes, Henriette."

"This does not upset you?"

"Should it?"

"Austria is your homeland, isn't it?"

1

The Queen didn't answer and motioned for her stunned lady-in-waiting to leave.

In the days and months that followed, Marie Antoinette clung to the hope that her former countrymen would come to her rescue. From her rooms in the *Tuileries Palace*, she set about a bold scheme to bring down France. She secretly wrote to her nephew, the Emperor of Austria, leaking detailed accounts of French military plans.

As the war raged on and Marie Antoinette sat in the hope of their anticipated rescue, she turned for solace to her children. Young Louis Charles had just turned seven, and she anxiously watched over him, sternly reminding his governess that they were after all still raising the future King.

But outside the walls of the stately prison, the radicals who wanted to put an end to the monarchy, began taking control of the Revolution. They fought for liberty, equality, and freedom and, on one late afternoon, some twenty thousand armed men stormed the *Tuileries* palace and compelled the royal family to submit.

Forced into captivity in the Temple fortress, on September 21, 1792, King Louis XVI and Queen Marie Antoinette of France became nothing more than ordinary citizens of the new French Republic. The monarchy, which had endured for nearly one thousand years, was now no more.

. . .

From inside the fortress, Marie Antoinette stared across the Paris rooftops from the one small narrow window of their prison room. The light breeze carried a strong scent of lavender that had her inhale deeply. She longed to run her palms across the light purple bristles in her cherished palace garden in Versailles—a far cry from the Temple's inner courtyard that never saw the sun. Confined to the gloomy medieval fortress in the middle of Paris, she had lost all hope of being freed. France was still at war against Austria, and now with Russia's aid, defeat was imminent but nowhere in sight.

The heavy wooden door to the room flung open behind her.

"Sire, they're coming for you!" one of the loyal staff warned the King.

Marie Antoinette watched as her husband remained seated in the wake of the attendant's words. From the empty corridors, the loud thumping of the guards' feet drew nearer and nearer. King Louis knew what was to come since his short trial had offered little chance of acquittal. Facing his fate, he gathered his two young children into a final embrace. Louis Charles' big blue eyes filled with tears and his older sister clung desperately to her father's arm.

"If this is the last time we see each other, God be with you. You reigned with honor and courage," Marie Antoinette whispered.

"I regret that my lot has subjected you to this much grief, my Queen. It has afforded you a great injustice, and for that, I humbly seek your forgiveness."

Moments later their solemn farewell was disrupted as six guards stormed into the room, their swords drawn. King Louis XVI had been found guilty of treason and sentenced to death by guillotine. Louis did not resist when they tied his hands behind his back. His eyes remained fixed on his wife's until they swung him around and pushed him toward the exit.

At ten thirty in the morning, on January 21, 1793, the sound of rolling drums announced to the Queen that her husband was dead.

And just as she was once thrust into her reign, her eight-year-old son, to those who still believed in the monarchy, became the new heir to a throne he would never own.

JULY 3, 1793 - SIX MONTHS LATER

"Mama! Don't let them take me!"

Marie Antoinette stared into her young son's big blue eyes. The sharp pain that lay across her chest threatened to break her heart in two.

"Leave him alone. Where are you taking him?" she cried.

But the four swordsman gave her no regard and pushed her to the floor.

"Mama! I don't want to go!"her son yelled repeatedly as the men dragged him away.

Helpless and distraught Marie Antoinette covered her ears with her shawl in a futile attempt to block out her boy's anguished screams that filled the empty passages in the Temple until they eventually faded in the distance.

The pain in her chest had become a dull heavy ache that left her body numb to the cold floor she still lay on. She didn't care if she got ill or died. She had nothing more to live for. Not even her daughter's soft cries at her side consoled her broken heart. Regret tormented her soul. It had been three years since they stormed the Palace and destroyed everything she once held dear. Filled with misery and despair, her thoughts trailed back to that fateful time that marked the day their lives changed forever.

OCTOBER 1789, FRANCE - THREE YEARS EARLIER

As the large iron gates swung shut behind them, they turned and looked at Versailles for the last time. The horseman flicked the reins hard, slapping loudly against his horses' backs and bawled out a strident command for them to move faster. Marie Antoinette pulled her two young children closer to her side. Opposite her in the carriage, her husband stared blankly out in front of him displaying no emotion whatsoever.

Filled with anguish, the once loved Queen continued to

search her husband's eyes. Fear and uncertainty flooded the pit of her stomach. For the first time since their elaborate wedding, desperate to escape their dire situation, she looked to him for guidance. But, as anticipated, his eyes revealed nothing. It came as no surprise to her that he showed no inclination to remedy the circumstances they now found themselves in. She had always been the instigator in their royal affairs—something her mother intentionally educated and prepared her for from a very young age.

Her husband of nearly two decades had never really been a man of much courage or strength even though he was the King of France. She supposed it was to be expected since he had been thrust into the role at only nineteen years of age. As if he read her thoughts, King Louis XVI pushed his chin out and upwards, suddenly showing more grit than she had ever seen in him before. She knew at that moment that it was merely his desperate attempt to keep up appearances to his outraged subjects who lined the narrow road. Marie Antoinette forced down a wave of nausea. Once the revered King and Queen of France, their fate was now in the hands of the angry mob that flanked the carriage and forced them from their lavish palace home.

As they rode further along the road, a tall tree's auburn leaves wafted on the tailcoats of the cool autumn breeze and landed on the carriage floor beside her feet. She had a sudden urgency to savor the experience for fear of it being the last time she would ever have the privilege of breathing in her beloved fresh countryside air. The modest horse carriage rolled down the road, and in its pursuit, thousands of angry men and woman waved their pitchforks, broom handles and kitchen knives in the air.

"I'll have her heart displayed on my nightstand!" one of the women shouted in anger. "I'll take her head!" another added, cheered on by the rest of the mob.

Marie Antoinette pressed her young daughter's head against her chest, shielding her from the ferocious onslaught of unceasing insults that trailed behind them. At only eleven years of age, Marie Thérèse's terrified eyes took hold of her mother's. Filled with questions entwined with fear and lack of life experience, she silently begged her mother to tell her that it had all just been a horrible nightmare. But it wasn't, and instead, Marie Antoinette gently patted her daughter's arm in silent reply. For the moment Marie Antoinette found solace in the fact that at least her daughter's life ought not to be in danger. As a princess, she was exempt from inheriting the crown— unlike the destiny that befell her younger brother.

Marie Antoinette numbed her ears from the hateful women's slanderous threats and turned her attention to her four-year-old son who, unbeknownst to him yet, would bear the hate of the people for years to come. As the sole heir to the French throne, he would become the next king should death befall his father. She cursed his undeserved fate and brushed an auburn lock from his pale face. His rosy lips turned upward into a slight smile, and his big blue eyes declared his naivety of the situation at hand. Perhaps God will grant him compassion and spare his life, she thought.

The rider cracked his whip over his horses' heads and pushed them forward down the winding gravel road. As the carriage gained speed, the Palace of Versailles slowly disappeared behind the trees. Without knowledge of where they were taking them, fear overcame the Queen, and the thought of losing her children twisted her stomach in a knot. She knew all too well what it meant to lose a child. She had buried two already. It had only been two years since her infant daughter went on to meet her maker and a mere four months since tuberculosis claimed the life of their first-born son. She stared out into the autumn-kissed countryside. Louis Joseph was only eight years old when the sickness claimed his life. As the eldest son, he was to inherit the crown from his father when the time came. She brushed a solitary tear from her cheek and looked at her youngest son next to her. Fate had stepped in and forced its hand on him instead. Louis Charles would be next in line to the throne.

As the incensed mob's cries grew faint with the distance now increasing between them, the King's previous upright demeanor eventually changed and he dropped his head forward into his hands as his emotions finally got the better of him.

"I should have listened to you, my Queen. I'm so sorry. You were right. Now my foolishness has caused this family great distress."

"It's not your fault. You couldn't have known this would happen," the wretched King's wife consoled him, even though she deeply regretted not forcing him to go along with her plans to escape to Austria. It had been several months since the people of France attacked the Bastille. Now, their attention had turned on what they'd directed their hatred toward all along—the Queen of France.

Yes, Marie Antoinette knew she was mostly to blame for this unfortunate event. Her extravagant lifestyle, parties, and gambling addiction had blinded her from seeing the suffering of the poverty-stricken French people. Years of harbored resentment had them taking revenge on her fool-ishness and disinclination to rule as a Queen was supposed to. They hated her. She had seen the obscene pamphlets that falsely accused her of living a life indulging in sensual plea-sures while secretly entertaining male suitors behind the palace walls. Neither of which was true, but they had convicted her and found her guilty without trial or debate. That she enjoyed getting dressed up in the most exquisite jewels and silks and hosted many lavish garden parties, that fact was true. But she had always been faithful to her husband even though he'd never loved her. If only her mother were alive to see what she had forced her daughter's hand into. Marie Antoinette had never wanted to leave Austria and be married off to a future king, much less at an age a mere two years older than her daughter currently was.

The twelve miles from Versailles to Paris felt like an eter-nity and for the most part, remained peaceful with only a few passing peasants attacking them with stones. But as they neared the *Tuileries Palace,* the crowds made it nearly impossible for the carriage to move freely. Once again, the people shouted angry abuse at the royal family, driving their pitchforks and pikes into the sides of the coach. A few of the noblemen who had turned against the crown urged the crowds to be patient.

"Let them through! They can rule over you no more! The time has come for them to feel your suffering. From now on, they will do as we dictate!"

The crowd roared in agreement, parting to allow the carriage to enter the gates to the once primary residence of the monarchy. Under heavy guard, King Louis XVI, Queen Marie Antoinette, and their two young children became the very thing the quisling noblemen had promised the Parisian people—a powerless King and Queen held prisoner by their once loyal subjects.

♟

Held captive and under constant guard in the modest palace, their lifestyle had been reduced to one of simplicity. A far cry from the luxury and freedom they'd experienced in Versailles the royal family filled their days strolling through the small gardens or reading in their humble quarters. Beyond the palace walls, the people continued their fight to bring down the monarchy. Their once noble entourage's heads, planted on pikes, decorated the city square and the fight for liberty and freedom grew more intense as the days passed.

Marie Antoinette became more anxious and fragile by the day. There were times her intense fear had her crying hysterically. She didn't fear death for herself. Instead, the thought of her children facing the same fate, or worse being orphaned and left desolate to fend for themselves, was what had left her paralyzed. Desperate to distract her mind from their confinement, the Queen began to work on large pieces of tapestry. With her mind too much occupied with surrounding dangers, the needle was the only vocation that could divert her. The more awful her life became, the steelier she was and the harder she bravely fought back against their imprisonment. The sole topic of her discourse was the Revolution. She sought to discover the real opinions the Parisians had of her and wondered how she had lost the affection they once held for her.

With the King in a constant state of dormancy, the Queen was determined to win back the monarchy and set out to work against the Revolution. She secretly took council from ambassadors and advisors and learned to read and write in code to communicate with allies in other countries.

But even their near successful escape proved futile in changing the grim future that awaited the once Royal Family of France.

CHAPTER ONE

P resent day— London

    Alex gasped for air when they finally pulled her head out from underneath the water. It stung deep in the back of her nose where the cold liquid forced its way into her lungs. Several times she coughed hard in an anguished attempt to expel the water from her lungs, but it didn't help much. Desperate to gain control, she calmed her mind. She knew it wouldn't take long before they shoved her head under the water again. With her mind racing against time, she fought to calm her breathing and restore oxygen to her lungs, all the while wriggling her wrists under the strain of the cable ties that had her hands restrained behind her back.

"Who are you?" She spoke in a strained voice.

"None of your concern. Now, do we make ourselves clear?" one of the men behind her answered.

Alex tried to agree, but her air pipe was still waterlogged, and instead, she coughed and turned her head sideways to loosen the grip they had on her hair. Something she instantly realized was a mistake when they misinterpreted her reaction as defiance. The force of the men's hands on the back of her head signaled for her to draw a quick deep breath a split second before they pushed her head under the water again. This time she decided to save her energy and not fight it. She shut her eyes tight and tried to remain calm. They weren't there to kill her, that much she knew. They could have easily done so already if they wanted to.

Her lungs hurt as they strained under the lack of oxygen she so sorely needed. She knew she was almost at capacity, and as if they read her mind, they pushed her head down even deeper under the water. Alex opened her eyes, instantly regretting when the water stung behind her eyeballs. They had added bath salt to aid the torture. It worked. She felt as if her lungs were going to explode. Liquid pushed in through her nostrils setting off the impulse to pull her head out of the water, only to again become aware of their forceful hands behind her head. Her body kicked into fight mode, and she pushed her knees down hard onto the floor. Her hips thrust forward into the side of the bath, and she forced her shoulders back against their strong hands. Her neck ached as she pushed her head back and sideways in a desperate attempt to get her mouth above the water level. The sudden defiance caught her attackers off guard, and one of the men's feet slipped on the wet floor, sending him flat onto the tiles behind her. The instant relief from her attacker's hand on the back of her head afforded her a brief chance to draw in a deep breath and push herself away from the bath. The floor was slippery beneath her tennis shoes, and with her hands tied behind her back, made it impossible for her to attempt an escape. The second man yanked back hard on her hair and dragged her sideways across her bathroom floor.

Still trying to recover from near drowning, she yelped a soft cry as her hair pulled at her scalp. She walked her feet backward in her attacker's direction, attempting to alleviate some of the tension on her scalp, but the man yanked harder and dragged her onto her knees to face him. She studied his shoes. Judging from his skillful torture method, she'd assumed he'd be wearing black combat boots but instead he wore polished tan leather shoes and taupe suit trousers. Confused, she tried to look up at his face, but he pushed her head down, forcing her to remain kneeling with her eyes facing the floor. She did as he demanded and suddenly became aware of someone else walking behind her. She was certain two men had held her down in the bath, and both of them stood in front and to her left. It was apparent there must be a third attacker in the room. She waited on her knees with her gaze downward, taking in every sight, sound, and smell.

"Who are you? What do you want?" She attempted again.

Her question went unanswered. Instead, Alex felt the sharp sting of her attacker's hand against her cheekbone. The thrust only pushed her slightly off balance but deciding to seize the moment, she amplified her fall and intentionally swung her body around. She caught a glimpse of a well-dressed man staring out the bathroom window with his back toward her.

Her dirty tactic angered her attacker, and he kicked at her lower back, slamming her face hard into the tiled floor. Blood ran from her nose. She pinched her eyes shut trying to absorb the pain while she tried sneaking a second look at the man by the window, but her attempt proved impossible from behind her tangled, wet hair that now formed a thick curtain around her head.

She listened closely when the man moved away from the window and leaned in. His raspy voice spoke close to her ear in a soft but urgent whisper.

"Stay out of our business or the next time we meet we'll kill you."

His words were barely cold when Alex felt a hard blow against the back of her head, and everything went black.

Afaint beeping sound grew louder and louder as Alex regained consciousness. She forced her heavy eyelids open and took in the blurry vision of a room that didn't look like the bathroom at her apartment anymore.

"Doctor, she's waking up," a female voice spoke next to her.

"Can you hear me?" a male voice added at her feet.

"Where am I?"

"You're in the hospital. Can you remember your name?"

"Alex."

"Good, and your last name?"

"Hunt."

"What year is it?"

"2019."

"How many fingers am I holding up?"

"Four."

He leaned in and shone a bright flashlight into each of her eyes and mumbled something to the nurse who responded by holding out two pills and a blue plastic cup with a straw.

A moment later, two men in black coats stood at her feet.

"Miss Hunt, I'm Chief Inspector Shawn McDowell from Scotland Yard. We need to ask you some questions, please?"

The nurse propped a pillow behind her back, and Alex nodded.

"Can you tell us what happened?"

Alex stared at the bald, middle-aged man with the red beard and strong Irish accent. A younger wide-eyed more handsome man stood next to him, ready with his black notebook and pen.

"Ma'am, can you remember what happened?"

Alex paused, gathering her words before she continued in a croaky voice.

"I arrived home from the office, and they were already inside my apartment."

She paused, searching through her blurry memory.

"Then what?"

"They grabbed me and tied my hands behind my back."

Alex swallowed as the events became less vague. She recalled hearing them fill her bath.

"They dragged me off to my bathroom and shoved my head under the water in my bath. I tried to fight them off and the next thing I knew I woke up here."

"Did you see how many there were?"

Alex nodded. "Three, I think."

"Did you see their faces?"

She shook her head in reply.

"Is there anything you can remember about the attackers? Clothes, shoes, scars, accents."

"They wore suits. Expensive suits. Couture and they had French accents."

"Outstanding Miss Hunt, what did they say to you?"

"Nothing much. I asked them what they wanted, and one of them just told me to stay out of their business, or they'd kill me."

"So they gave you a warning?"

"I guess so."

"Do you have any idea what they might have meant when they said you needed to 'stay out of their business'? What business might that be?"

"I have no idea, chief inspector. I've never met them before."

"How would you know if you never saw their faces?"

"Because they had French accents. I don't have any French-speaking clients."

"And what exactly is your line of business?"

"I'm an independent antiquities recoverer."

The inspector's assistant lifted his head from his notebook and looked at his boss. Visibly as confused as his sidekick, the chief inspector cleared his throat.

"So you restore antiques?"

"Not quite, I get hired to recover and return looted or lost artifacts after determining their authenticity and origin. I used to be an archaeologist."

"I see. Who hires you?"

"Governments, private museums, universities, private collectors, anyone really."

"So let me get this straight Miss Hunt. You're a relic hunter?"

Alex smiled. "No inspector. Treasure hunters find lost pirate treasures for personal financial gain. I recover historical artifacts that have gone missing or got stolen and return them to their original owners."

"I see. So would it be safe to say these artifacts are of great value then? Financially that is."

"Some of them, yes."

"Are you working on recovering anything of significance at the moment that might have triggered this attack?"

Alex reached for her plastic cup of water while rehearsing her answer in her head. She knew full well that in her line of business, there was high risk. As much as she'd like to find her assailants, getting the police involved now would prove detrimental.

"Nothing important enough to warrant someone breaking into my house and torturing me, no," she lied.

"They threatened to kill you, Miss Hunt. That sounds like a warning to me— a serious one at that."

Alex dropped her head back against her pillow. Her head hurt where they'd hit her.

"Inspector McDowell, I think that's enough for now. We'd be happy to make an appointment to come see you once she feels better, but for now, I think you've got enough to go on."

Alex instantly opened her eyes and sat up when she heard Sam's voice.

"And you are?" Inspector McDowell swung around to face Sam.

"Sam Quinn, Dr. Sam Quinn. Miss Hunt's former colleague and fiancée. I'm the one who found her and called the police."

"I see," said the inspector tapping his fingernails on the bed railing. "All right then. Thank you for your time, Miss Hunt. If you remember anything else, please let me know," the inspector added, handing her his business card before leaving the hospital room.

.   .   .

"Hey, how are you feeling? That was quite a knock to the head." Sam leaned in and planted a kiss on her forehead.

"I'm fine, honestly. In fact, you can hand me my clothes so we can get out of here," Alex replied, pulling back the hospital blanket.

"Uh-uh. Not so hasty, missy. You're not going anywhere just yet."

"I'm fine, Sam. It's just a bump."

"Not according to your file."

Sam had taken her hospital file from the wall above her head. "Says here you have fluid in your lungs and a concussion; quite a serious one too. Get back to bed."

"Yes, well, I feel fine. I can rest at home."

"You and I both know that won't happen." Sam's tone turned more serious. "They almost killed you, Alex."

"If they wanted to kill me, they could have. They didn't. Trust me. This will all blow over."

Sam walked across to the door and closed it behind him.

"Okay, out with it. What's really going on here?"

"What do you mean? Nothing is going on. I told the police

the truth. And why exactly is Scotland Yard involved in this anyway?"

"Good question," Sam answered, "the police found evidence beyond their jurisdiction. No idea what. They won't tell me."

Sam pulled Alex's legs back onto the bed and under the covers before propping himself onto the bed next to her.

"I've known you long enough to know you're hiding something, Alex. These guys meant business. If I hadn't stopped by, you'd still be lying unconscious on your bathroom floor. I'm still not convinced it is wise for you to run this business on your own. It's not safe."

"Not this again, Sam. I thought we'd settled this."

"That was before you got tortured and left for dead. I'd say that changes things. You should consider taking the ICCRU position, Alex. It's safer."

"What, and sit bored stiff behind a desk all day? No, thank you. I didn't work this hard to play it safe. Besides, I only got blindsided because I had my mind occupied with the wedding. Once that's over, I'll be back to my old self. I still think we should just elope."

"You're avoiding the question. What are you working on, Alex?"

Sam was right. He knew her too well.

"I can't tell you. It's classified."

"That's a load of crock if ever I heard any. You work for yourself Alex. Last time I checked you didn't have anyone else you needed to run anything by."

"I can't tell you, Sam. It's for your own protection. You're going to have to trust me."

"So there is more to this than you're letting on, isn't there?"

Alex refrained from answering.

Knowing full well her stubborn nature would merely push her further away if he persisted, Sam moved over to the recliner in the corner and settled down into it.

"Well, I'll wait it out. I'm not letting you out of my sight for a second, and just so you know, I have some torture tactics of my own. Don't make me use them."

Alex laughed. "So you're staying here now?"

"Yep and when you get discharged, you're staying at my place until they catch the guys."

"Nice try, but we're not yet married Sam Quinn."

CHAPTER TWO

When Alex and Sam walked into her top floor apartment a few days later, the place had been turned upside down.

"Was it like this when you found me?"

"You mean, ransacked? No, they must have come back," Sam answered while doing a quick sweep of the rest of the apartment.

"They were looking for something. All the cupboards are open. What do you think they're after?"

"Not sure, Sam. Can't say I have anything of interest here."

"And at the office?"

"Don't think so either."

"Well, there's no doubt in my mind they were looking for something. It's obvious they think you have it."

Sam looked at Alex where she stood behind her Edwardian roll-top desk in the corner of the sitting room.

"This isn't going to blow over Alex, and you know it. Whatever you've gotten yourself into, you can't pursue it on your own. It's too dangerous."

Sam paused, placing one hand on his hip.

"I'm going to resign from the uni and team up with you."

"That's the most ridiculous thing I've ever heard, Sam. I'm quite capable of looking after myself, you know. Not to mention the fact that we have our wedding around the corner. How are we supposed to afford the huge guest list your mother wants? I can't pay you what the uni does."

Sam moved over to Alex and cupped her bruised face. "Your safety is more important to me than my mother's guest list, Alex. I'll have a word with her. Heck, we'll elope like you want to, but I'm not prepared to trade your life just so my mother can invite all their country club friends to our wedding. Now let me in and tell me what this is all about."

Alex stared into Sam's dark, comforting eyes. Feeling secure with him was effortless. She trusted him completely, and they had always worked well together. It would be effortless to tell him everything, but that would put his life at risk too, and she would never be able to live with herself if something happened to him.

She turned away from Sam and stared through the window blind's slats down into the street in front of her apartment building.

"Alex, talk to me. Please? I can't protect you if I don't know what you're involved in."

Without answering him, Alex suddenly stepped away from the window. She hastily pushed her desk to one side and flipped over the corner of the rug underneath it, catching Sam's feet as she did so. Stepping aside, Sam observed as she pushed down onto the floorboard. A barely audible click sounded before a rectangular hatch in the floor released to reveal a metal safe filled to the rafters with an assortment of weapons. Stunned into silence, Sam watched in awe as Alex retrieved two Colt XSE's, clicking their loaded magazines in place before putting one in the front of her waistband and the other in the small of her back. Next, she slipped a Glock 17 inside her ankle boot and pulled out a black backpack from the bottom of the box.

"Who *are* you?" Sam asked as he watched his fiancée transform into someone representative of an undercover MI6 operative.

"Here, take these. "She handed him two Berettas before flipping open a smaller box and retrieving several passports and bundles of cash.

"Seriously? Have you turned into a secret government agent or something? And where did you get all this money?"

"Hurry, we don't have much time."

"What? Why? What's happening?"

Alex ignored him as she disappeared down the passage into her bedroom and came back with two black hooded jackets.

She threw the larger one against Sam's chest. "Put this on and zip it up with the hood over your head," she said as she slipped into the smaller one.

Doing as he was told, he put the jacket on and looked down at what appeared to be more like a shiny tight-fitting wetsuit than a designer item. "Not quite my idea of a fashion statement but all right then."

"It's a bulletproof jacket, Sam. Now let's go!"

"Why would we need bulletproof jackets? Who are we running from, Alex? What's going on?" Sam probed as he followed her back into the bedroom.

"There's no time to explain, Sam. Just trust me. We need to get out of here."

The tension in Alex's voice was enough to let Sam know she wasn't fooling around and he followed her as she climbed through the bedroom window facing the back of the apartment out onto a narrow Juliette balcony Sam knew hadn't been there before. As puzzled as he was, he didn't argue. He trusted her.

Alex slid her fingers into the grid openings of a nearby air vent in the wall and as she did this, a rope ladder dropped from the roof above their heads.

"Unbelievable, when did you do all this?" Sam prodded for an answer, but Alex was already halfway up the ladder and onto the roof.

"Hurry!" she shouted down at him, and once Sam made it onto the roof next to her, she pulled him down beside her. "Stay down."

As quickly as the ladder appeared, it retracted back into place the instant Alex pulled back another hidden lever from inside the gutter.

"Now what?"

"See that door over there? It'll take you down to the boiler room. Keep your head down."

"And you?"

"Right behind you, now go!"

Sam didn't hesitate to do as she told him even though he felt he had no idea who this woman he thought he knew and loved had morphed into. But trusting her came easy. Something told him she knew exactly what she was doing, and that was all he needed to know, for now.

Sam crouched down and bolted for the door while Alex made her way to the front of the building and carefully popped her head over the ledge. In the street outside her apartment, the black sedan was still there, and a little further down the road, another two had arrived and parked up. As six armed men got out from their cars and crossed the street into her apartment building, she turned and headed for the door to the boiler room from where she and Sam exited shortly after into the road behind the building.

"This way." Alex motioned for Sam to follow her to where a dirt bike stood hidden underneath a silver tarp.

"Of course," Sam commented with sarcasm. "Any other surprises you want to spring on me today?"

"Nope, but I'd get on if I were you."

W hen the pair eventually approached Sam's apartment, Alex circled the block twice before finally bringing the bike to a stop.

"You'd be better off at your parents' house, Sam. You were seen entering my apartment with me, so you're not safe here. It's a matter of time before they find you. You have to leave right away and watch your back. Don't go anywhere else, got it?"

"And what about you? You're insane if you think I'm going

to leave you on your own. We have to go to the police. You're in over your head, Alex. We've been in many sticky situations, but my gut tells me this one is different."

Alex kissed her fingers and touched Sam's mouth through the opening of his helmet. "I love you Sam, but this mission might get you killed, and for that, I'm not prepared. I'll be back in time for the wedding. Promise."

Before Sam could argue, the sound of an automatic weapon rang through the air, and several bullets whooshed over their heads.

"Get on!" Alex yelled at Sam and opened the bike's throttle, almost throwing Sam off the back. A succession of bullets rained through the air, exploding through the windows of several parked cars on the side of the road. Sirens and horns set off a cacophony of noise in its wake.

The bike sped off away from the fast-approaching black vehicle behind them. Alex dropped a gear and was just about to turn the corner when the second vehicle surprised them from the front.

"Watch out!" Sam yelled. "Over there! Turn right!"

Alex followed his instruction and turned up a narrow side street. The motorbike's powerful engine roared between the buildings as she gained speed halfway up the road. In her wing mirror, Alex spotted the black car behind them. Directly ahead a civilian car slowly rolled down the street toward them. Alex searched for an out when she realized she had been riding against the traffic down a one-way street. She swerved onto the pavement, missing a parked car by a fraction and almost hit a young student who, with his back toward them and his headphones on, was oblivious to the danger unfolding around him.

Behind them, the chasing vehicle had been blocked off by the approaching car and, with nowhere to go, was forced to cease the pursuit.

"Can you see the third car anywhere?" Alex shouted back at Sam as she maneuvered the bike back onto the street and prepared to take a left.

"There's a third car?"

Sam had hardly uttered the words when the third black sedan turned in behind them and fired off several gunshots in their direction. The roads were crammed with pedestrians as they approached the busier part of the City along the River Thames. Panicked screams echoed through the air. Being there placed every one of those innocent people at risk. Not to mention that the commotion would undoubtedly attract the police. She had to divert and get out of there.

"Hold on!" she yelled, barely giving Sam enough notice to comply before bringing the bike to a dead halt. Almost as suddenly, she spun the bike around on its front wheel, stopped, and faced the chasing vehicle head-on. With one hand on the handlebars, she pulled her gun from her waist and fired a bullet directly into the front wheel of the shooters' car. As intended the tire exploded rendering the vehicle out of control and crashing it sideways into a parked car.

Police sirens shrieked through the air as the law finally caught up with them, and Alex sped off away from the scene. But they were outnumbered and out of time. Law enforcement vehicles had already surrounded the entire block. Out of options, she brought the bike to a slow halt and stopped, her eyes frantically searching for an escape route, but there was none. Behind them, more police chased after the shooters who had bolted in the opposite direction. Nearby, onlookers stood huddled around the first responders, already offering their account of the events they'd witnessed, and it wasn't long before a few of them pointed at Alex and Sam.

Panic engulfed Alex's insides as her eyes skimmed over the people and surrounding police vehicles for a way out.

"There's no way out, Alex," Sam said, sensing her plan to escape. "You do know the police are on our side. We've done nothing wrong."

"I don't know that, Sam. No one can be trusted."

"You can trust me."

"That's not in dispute here, Sam. It's bigger than any of this."

"What is, Alex? You're not making sense."

"Switch off your engine and place your hands above your

heads!" the police shouted from behind. A quick glimpse in the side-view mirror confirmed they had sneaked up behind them.

Sam's hands immediately lifted above his head while he started his dismount.

"I said, switch off the engine and put your hands above your head!"

But not even the second warning made Alex respond.

"Do as the man says, Alex," Sam urged while backing away from the motorcycle toward the police officer.

With the policeman's attention now on Sam, Alex seized the moment and dropped the bike's gear into first before launching the machine forward. Within seconds she blasted through a nearby small group of onlookers, forcing them to scatter out of the way. Knowing full well the police couldn't shoot into the crowds, she continued along the sidewalk between the panicked people and further away from where the policeman was arresting Sam.

Sam's eyes remained pinned on Alex as he watched her swerve the bike in between the crowds and eventually around two police cars that tried to barricade her in at the bottom of the street. Livid at her foolishness, he couldn't help but be equally proud of her audacious escape—the very quality he most loved about her. He should have seen it coming. But amidst his love and admiration, he felt over-whelming fear not knowing what secret she felt compelled to keep from him or who she was so desperate to get away from. All he knew with certainty was that he'd never before seen her quite as determined or as scared.

And as Alex disappeared around the next corner, leaving Sam to explain it all to the police, life on London's streets carried on as if nothing had happened.

CHAPTER THREE

S am sat squashed between two vagrants on the narrow
steel bench inside the holding cell. They reeked of
alcohol, and their clothes carried a stench so foul it perme-
ated the tiny four by four lock-up.

The rest of the cramped space didn't offer any better
company. Three guys dressed to the rafters in studded black
leather jackets and pants, tattoos covering just about every
exposed part of skin on their bodies, sat staring at Sam from
the opposite bench. It was apparent Sam's skin-tight bulletproof jacket had caught their attention. One of them, osten-
sibly the ringleader, flicked his pierced tongue in and out of
his mouth mimicking that of a lizard's tongue when he'd be
sensing his surroundings. Sam shuffled uncomfortably. The
last thing he wanted now was to have to deal with three
snot-nosed twenty-somethings stuck in an identity crisis.

He'd have to play it cool and pray that his turn to make his one phone call came round quickly.

"Nice jacket," the young thug commented.

"Thanks."

"Looks like you're too old to wear it."

"Ok."

The thug smirked and turned to his buddies to rally some support.

"Take it off."

"Yeah, I don't think so mate."

"You don't think so?" He laughed, looking over his shoulders to his two sidekicks. "He doesn't think so," he said, encouraging the other two who laughed mockingly.

He flicked his tongue again and got to his feet, his two friends in tow.

"Take it off, *mate.*"

Sam ignored his demand.

It angered the guy, and Sam watched as he took the two steps toward him, joined a second later by his friends. Sam remained seated and continued to ignore him.

"You should've taken it off when I asked nicely."

"Or else?"

The punk wrapped his fists below the collar on either side of the zip in Sam's jacket. In a weak attempt to pull Sam to his feet, it was apparent that the thug had underestimated Sam's height and athleticism. Annoyed, the bully heaved and shoved his flat hands against Sam's chest before falling back in line with his cronies. Sam, who was still seated, smiled and looked dead into the pierced punk's eyes. It was then that the guy came face to face with Sam's towering height as Sam stood up and met the clique in the center of the cell, rising a full head and shoulders above all three of them. Conscious of an audience and having to maintain his pride, the gang leader looked at his sidekicks.

"Show the old man what happens when people don't obey me."

At the end of the bench, a short, stocky man dressed in a grey business suit spoke. "Give it up, boys. You can see this 'old man' can run circles around you."

"Shut up, fool. No one asked your opinion. Unless you also want a piece of me?"

"Don't say I didn't warn you," the businessman added.

"What are you waiting for? Show him not to mess with me!" The punk shouted to his entourage, who stood frozen with hesitation in front of Sam.

The first youngster flicked his long, bleached, side-swept bangs out of his eyes as if it somehow gave him more courage. Two tattooed fists moved in front of his face as he readied himself to throw the first punch.

As with his leader, he too was much shorter than Sam. Nonetheless, acting on his orders, he courageously threw his fist out toward Sam's face. It took hardly any effort or preparation for Sam to casually move his head sideways, ducking the pathetic attempt at a punch with ease.

Another punch thrust forward, and again, Sam ducked.

"Told you," the amused businessman piped up from the corner.

The two drunk vagrants started cheering for Sam joined in by an apron-wearing hawker who, until now, had sat quietly observing.

"My money's on the tall guy," the hawker shouted in a strong Hindu accent.

Excitement filled the holding cell as the second punk joined his friend, entirely missing Sam's face when Sam side-stepped again to escape his incoming punch.

"Idiots!" the gang leader scoffed.

Several more attempts were flung toward Sam, who maintained his calm composure and didn't fight back.

Each time the two leather-clad punks missed or fell to the ground as Sam dodged their attacks, their small prison audience roared with laughter.

"Give it to them, lad. These kids need to be taught a lesson," the toothless vagrants cheered Sam on. But true to Sam's unaggressive nature, he never once raised his fists, resolved to only defend by blocking the punches and stepping out of their way.

The trio soon tired, and their lack of support from the fellow inmates didn't help.

"Told you so, knucklehead. Give it up and get back on your bench," the businessman intervened.

His rebuke infuriated the troublemaker who, by now, had not a shred of pride left in him. Without warning, he turned and punched the businessman full on the nose.

"Who's an idiot now, huh?"

"Back off, kid." Sam spoke for the first time and gripped the young man's arms firmly behind his back. "You've had your fun now sit down and give it a rest."

Defeated and stripped of all dignity, the punk straightened his jacket and grudgingly complied.

"You ok?" Sam asked the businessman who wiped the blood from his nose and answered with annoyance. "Bloody punks. Streets are full of them."

"Sam Quinn," said Sam, holding out his hand.

"Fitz. Actually it's Dennis Fitzgerald the third, but everyone just calls me Fitz."

"Nice to meet you, Fitz. What brings you here?"

"My ex. The woman is hellbent on destroying my life. Accused me of stalking when all I wanted to do was watch my boy play football."

"That's a tough spot. Sorry to hear." Sam took a seat next to Fitz.

"Take it from me, my friend. Never get married. Women are trouble." Fitz wiped a bead of sweat from his forehead before continuing. "So what are you in for?"

Sam let out a chuckle. "Ironically, also a woman."

"How else? I tell you, my friend, I've had it with women. Never thought I'd say it, but I'm done. Here, take my card. I'll hook you up with the best divorce attorney in the country. I sold his London apartment some time back. One of the best I tell ya," and handed Sam a business card.

Sam studied the platinum embossed realtor card and slipped it in his pocket.

"So you're a realtor?"

"High-end residential apartments— the best in the business. I have clients from here to Dubai. I don't ask where their money comes from and they like that. Keeps me in business and helps me keep the ex off my back. As long as I pay each month, she lets me see my boy. What do you do? Let me guess. Judging from how you handled these punks

I'd say you're some socialite's head of security or something."

Sam laughed. "Now there's an idea. Afraid not though."

"Quinn, you're free to go," a policeman interrupted as he summoned from the cell door, surprising Sam with the announcement.

"Good on you, mate. Ring me up and don't let her mess you around, you hear me?"

"Cheers, Dennis Fitzgerald the third. I'll see you around."

S am followed the constable down the long hallway. "Who posted bail?" he asked.

"No one, You're free to go. After your interrogation, that is."

Confused at his last words Sam followed the guard into a nearby interrogation room where he was told to sit at a small white table in the middle of the floor, after which the constable disappeared closing the door behind him. Across the room, Sam's reflection stared back at him from a mirrored wall. He had watched enough crime programs on the telly to know this was a one-way mirror. He didn't yet know who was on the other side of that mirror and why, but he was sure to find out soon enough.

The door opened, and a slim brunette in a tight black suit sat down at the table opposite him. She placed a yellow folder marked 'classified' on the table but kept it closed and folded her hands on top of it.

"Mr. Quinn, can I get you a cup of coffee, tea, maybe some water?"

"Coffee sounds great, thanks. And it's Dr. Quinn."

"Yes, of course, sorry. Force of habit. I'm DC Morgan. Would you mind if I asked you a few questions about the incident earlier?"

"I'd rather speak to Chief Inspector McDowell from Scotland Yard."

Sam's request left her pausing briefly. A glance in the mirror behind her confirmed Sam's earlier suspicions.

"Chief Inspector McDowell. Right, and what might your interest be in speaking with him?"

"He'll know."

"Dr. Quinn, perhaps I can be of service in the interim. Can you tell me what you were doing chasing through the streets this morning?"

"I wasn't aware I was chasing anything?"

The detective constable's eyes revealed her annoyance at Sam's smart answer.

"Can you tell me why you were *being* chased this morning?"

"Miss Morgan, I mean no disrespect, but chasing or being chased, hypothetically speaking, isn't a crime. What are you charging me with?"

"We're not charging you, yet, Dr. Quinn. This is merely an investigation as to what happened this morning and why you were involved."

"Well, in that case, I'm free to go."

"Not quite, we also arrested two other men involved in the chase known to be involved in several open Interpol cases."

Sam's heart skipped a beat. He assumed she was referring to the shooters who had been after Alex.

"Do you know them?"

"No, should I?"

"Perhaps."

"I don't."

"We have several reports from witnesses saying they were shooting at you."

"Not that I know of. I'm very much alive, aren't I?"

"Then why were they chasing you?"

Sam shrugged his shoulders. "Who said they were?"

"All right." She cleared her throat and continued. "Who was with you on the motorbike?"

"What motorbike?"

"Quit playing games, Dr. Quinn. You were seen being chased and shot at through the streets of London on the back of a motorbike. One that wasn't driven by you. Who was it?"

"I don't know. Someone who offered me a lift to work."

"A lift to work," she repeated.

"Uh-huh."

"How did it come about that this person offered you a lift to work?"

"I missed the bus and decided to hitch a ride."

"So this guy on the bike stopped and picked you up."

"Precisely."

DC Morgan sat back in her chair and crossed her arms.

"And this happened where?"

"Outside my apartment, I told you. I missed the bus, stuck my thumb out, and hitched a ride."

"You know you could have called a taxi or an Uber. Why didn't you?"

"I didn't think of it."

A policeman entered the interrogation room and placed a cup of coffee on the table in front of Sam.

Detective Constable Morgan flipped open her file and pulled out a color photo from the inside flap, placing it down in front of Sam.

"Are these yours?"

Sam took a sip of the coffee without answering.

"Why were you carrying these two Berettas?"

"I wasn't. They're not mine."

"Dr. Quinn, these are untraceable. Their serial numbers have been removed and we found them at the scene."

Caught off guard by the information Sam took in another mouthful of coffee. He had no idea why Alex had untraceable guns hidden under her floorboards. He remained silent.

"Where did you get the guns, Dr. Quinn?"

"DC Morgan, they're not mine and since I haven't committed any crime or am I under arrest, I'd like to leave now."

The detective slipped the photo back into the file and slammed it shut.

"You're free to go Dr. Quinn, but so that you know, we're watching you."

Sam rose from his chair and walked toward the door, briefly looking back to see DC Morgan staring, arms folded, into the one-way mirror. There was a lot more to this interrogation than he'd learned today. Someone behind that mirror was pulling her strings.

He closed the door behind him and paused outside in the passageway. The door to the next room opened, and a medium built man in a three-piece suit holding an antique silver cane stepped out. Their eyes met, and Sam got the distinct impression the man had every intention of being seen. The intimidating look in his eyes was every bit intended to be a silent warning. To what, remained to be seen.

CHAPTER FOUR

S am walked briskly toward the nearest subway entrance —his mind laden with unanswered questions. Alex was in trouble, real trouble, and he wasn't even sure she knew just how much danger she was in. Or did she? Could it be the very reason she didn't want to tell him? To protect him from getting involved? In the back of his mind, he wondered if the police were in on it. It wouldn't be the first time he'd come face to face with corruption. Who was the man with the cane, and why was he part of the police investigation team?

He stopped at a crossing and waited for the light to change, joined by four other pedestrians also wanting to cross the street—a young couple, an exec on his phone and a guy on his late afternoon run. The pedestrian crossing light turned green, and the jogger hurriedly pushed past Sam, bumping him out of the way and into the exec.

"Watch it mate!" the irritated executive shouted after the jogger before returning to his phone conversation.

The subway buzzed with commuters on their travels home from work and Sam patiently waited in line at the turnstile. His hand slipped into his pants pocket in search of some coins and pulled out a single silver key instead. Puzzled, he stared at the unfamiliar object in his hand and read the inscription: one zero four. It wasn't his, and he had no idea how it got in his possession. He flipped it over to reveal the logo of a luxury hotel less than a mile from him. Most hotels used key cards so it couldn't be to a room. A locker, perhaps, he concluded. He stepped away from the line and proceeded down the street in the direction of the hotel.

A few blocks further on the lavish hotel's doorman tried hard to hide his uncertainty over whether Sam agreed with their clientele's profile or not, but opened the door and welcomed him in, nevertheless. A strong exotic scent wafted through the tranquil foyer—a clever marketing tactic to lure its guests to their on-site spa.

"Checking in, sir?" the overly friendly concierge enquired.

"Not just yet, but could you show me to your lockers, please," Sam said, holding up the key.

"Of course, sir. That will be in the fitness center, right this way."

Sam followed the polite man through the hotel foyer and into the in-house fitness center, where he paused outside the men's washrooms.

"You'll find the lockers inside, sir. Is there anything else I can help you with today?"

"No thanks, that's it for now."

And as quickly as he'd appeared, he turned and left.

Sam briefly paused when he turned the key in the lock. He had since figured out that it must have been the jogger at the crosswalk who'd slipped the key into his pocket. For a moment, the thought had crossed his mind that it might be a trap, or worse, a bomb meant to kill him. He shrugged off the absurd notion. As far as he knew he wasn't the one with the target on his back, Alex was. Still, his heart raced, and he took a deep breath as he pulled back on the key to open the locker. To his relief, nothing exploded in his face, nor could he hear any ticking sounds coming from the black gym bag that sat crammed into the small space in front of him.

He turned and looked over his shoulder to see if anyone was around. Pleased to see he was alone, he reached in and pulled the black bag from the locker. It weighed very little, and he set it down on a nearby wooden bench before carefully unzipping it. A silver-gray wig, matching fake mustache and a pair of sunglasses lay loosely on top of black sweatpants and matching hoodie. Underneath that was a single pair of sneakers with an envelope.

Intrigued by the surprise contents, he tore open the envelope to reveal a car key and a note that read,

> *Sam*
> *I'm sorry you were dragged into this. Fate played its hand and you are now in danger. Change into this disguise. Take the hired vehicle parked in the hotel parking and drive to your parents' seaside cottage—you should be safe there.*
> *A*

Sam stared at the note in his hand and dropped down onto the bench. Fear pulled his stomach into a tight knot making it hard to breathe. Through all the years of working together, this was the only time he had ever seen Alex go to such extreme lengths as using disguises and decoys—she wasn't one for the theatrical. Tiny beads of sweat broke out on his lip as he reread the note. If only he knew where she was, he could help her.

A nervous giggle erupted as he recalled how she had been the one to rescue him that morning. It certainly seemed he required her help instead of the other way around. She'd proved more than capable of looking after herself. He sat, staring at the note. What choice was there other than to comply and follow her instructions? He had no idea where to even start looking for her.

Suddenly conscious he might have been followed to the hotel he grabbed the bag and disappeared into the nearest cubicle. It took barely two minutes to change into the track-suit. He fumbled nervously with the wig deciding it might be better to adjust it in front of a mirror. Although he had been paying attention to anyone who might have walked into the changing rooms, he cautiously opened the cubicle door and briefly popped his head out to make sure he was still alone. He was and quickly moved across the floor to the mirror.

The odd colored wig with matching strip of hair on his lip and brown sunglasses made him look like a Vegas Elton John impersonator. All he needed was a gold earring dangling from his ear, he thought while he inspected the final product in the mirror.

Behind him, the door to the changing room opened to one of the cleaning staff, and he hurriedly snatched up the bag and headed to the parking garage.

Several vehicles were parked in front of him when the elevator doors opened into the basement parking. He looked at the key in his hand. He was looking for a Mercedes. His eyes skimmed over the pool of luxury cars, and he pressed down on the remote button. A double bleep accompanied by a quick show of spotlights drew his attention to a bay on his right.

"That was easy," he mumbled, making his way to the car.

It was eerily quiet. Sam wasn't one to scare in these situations, but given the circumstances, his nerves were on edge. Relieved when he reached the car, he sank into the leather seats behind the steering wheel and locked the doors. His eyes caught the written Post-it stuck on the rearview mirror, which simply read *glove box*. He flipped the glove compartment open to reveal a 9mm pistol. The mustache scratched against his cheeks when the corners of his mouth curled up. How typical for Alex to have all the angles covered.

I t was already dark when Sam arrived at his parents' seaside cottage on the south-east England coast. The bungalow sat on the water's edge and was reasonably secluded. He knew no one had followed him, but he was cautious and paused next to the car, peering out into the darkness. Everything was deathly silent.

As always, the spare key lay in its usual spot hidden under his mother's favorite pot plant around the back of the house. Any other time of the year his parents would have been at the cottage, but as it happened, they were in the throes of celebrating their thirty-fifth wedding anniversary on a Caribbean cruise ship. Inside, the house was quiet. The full moon still lay low over the ocean's horizon and shone its bright light into the open-plan sitting room. He left the lights' main switch off. Just in case. But it became evident very soon after that he was there on his own and there was no indication that Alex had been to the cottage at all. The thought of not knowing where she was or what trouble she was in left him anxiously pacing the front porch until well into the night.

He eventually dozed off in his father's recliner that stood in the small den that had spectacular views across the ocean. In the deep hours of the night, something woke him. Sure he heard a noise coming from the kitchen door behind him, he sat quietly listening. There it was again. Someone had entered the house. His hand tightened around the gun's handle that he had fallen asleep with and now lay in his lap. Sam listened as the floorboards creaked under the intruder's feet when he walked through the kitchen behind him.

Sam's temples throbbed under his pulsing heartbeat. His hand felt clammy against the pistol's stippled grip. With his other hand, he slowly stretched out to the nearby lamp, deciding he would surprise the prowler. Conscious of the intruder's whereabouts behind him, Sam readied himself. His stomach sank to his feet when he suddenly realized he hadn't switched on the electricity. But he quickly moved on to a plan B and quietly slid off the chair and onto the floor, hiding himself behind the recliner. The moonlight narrowly missed the chair, concealing Sam's hiding spot. When he cautiously popped his head out in an attempt to spot his visitor, there was no one there. A shred of doubt washed over him, but he quickly dismissed it when he heard the floorboards creaking in the bedroom. He straightened up and held the gun firmly out in front of his face.

His eyes searched the dark corners of the sitting room and then, he stealthily moved toward the corridor, careful not to trigger the squeaking floorboards under his feet. With his index finger barely touching the trigger, he lay his body back against the sitting room wall at the start of the corridor. He'd wait it out for the uninvited guest to come back down the passage and then surprise him from behind.

He waited, preparing himself for the possibility that it might be more than one intruder. It wasn't uncommon for burglars to prowl the small seaside village during the offseason. Most of the properties stood vacant this time of year.

The wooden floors warned him of the burglar's approach. Sam's arms and shoulders tensed up and he gripped the gun tighter. His reflexes kicked into high gear the moment he spotted a man wearing a dark hoodie moving past him. But the burglar was one up on Sam and instantly grabbed him by the arm and flung him forward over his shoulder, slamming Sam down on his back at his visitor's feet. The 9mm slid noisily across the floor and came to a halt against the kitchen island.

Determined to apprehend the intruder, Sam kicked the guy's feet out from under him which landed him face down onto the floor, affording Sam enough time to jump to his feet. Ready to throw the first punch, Sam took his boxing stance as the burglar followed suit.

At a good head and shoulders taller than his intruder Sam shouted, "Give it up, mate! There's nothing to steal here."

The burglar dropped his fists.

"Sam? It's me, Alex," she pushed her jacket's hood back.

"Alex? What are you doing sneaking up on me like that?"

"I might as well ask you the same thing, Sam. You could've shot and killed me!"

"Well, you did leave me the gun, and you did tell me to meet you here. Where have you been? I've been worried sick." He pulled her into his arms. "Are you okay?"

"I'm fine. What do you mean I told you to meet me here?"

"The note, the ridiculous disguise, the rental at the hotel."

Sam paused when the moon shone across her stunned face. "Wait, you don't know what I'm talking about, do you? I don't understand Alex. Someone slipped me a key to a locker in the Hilton which had a bag with a disguise and a note from you saying I should meet you here."

"I didn't send you a note, Sam. It wasn't me. I received one too, simply telling me to come here and to wait for further instructions."

Alex started pacing, biting her thumb as she often still did.

"Well, then who did? Alex, what on earth is going on? What's with all this secrecy? Who's after you?"

CHAPTER FIVE

"I have no idea, Sam. I've been trying to figure it out myself."

It was Sam's turn to pace the room.

"Why don't you start from the beginning, Alex? Whoever set this up did their homework. How else would they know to send us here? Better yet, why? We're almost two hours out of London, and why involve me now? I mean, it's not like we work together anymore."

Alex walked out onto the deck overlooking the ocean, desperate for the fresh night air to clear her mind that was now racing with questions.

"I don't know Sam. I'm not sure you were supposed to even be involved—at least not by whoever's been sending me these messages."

"What messages?"

Alex sighed, reasoning that it was probably unavoidable not to let Sam in on everything at this stage.

"It started about a month ago. I received an anonymous letter through the letterbox at my apartment. It stated only my name. No return address, no sender's details, nothing. Just a plain typed up envelope with the letter inside."

"Go on."

"He asked for my help. Said I was the only one he could turn to, and that he'd guide me through the entire process. He'd protect me but said that I couldn't tell anyone. I had to burn the letter and wait for further instructions."

"Help with what? Protect from whom?"

"I have no idea!" she blurted out with a combination of fear and frustration in her voice. "At first I didn't make anything of it. I thought it was just a prank by those silly teenagers next door. But then a couple of days later I got the bag with guns, money and counterfeit passports for both of us. Then I came home one day and, out of thin air the balcony with instructions on how to escape through it had mysteriously attached itself to the wall outside my window. A week later, someone slipped the next letter under my door at the office."

"Did you manage to see who delivered it?"

"I got to the door too late."

"What did it say?"

"Nothing, there was no note, just a newspaper cutting dated June 9, 1795."

"1795! You mean to say it was an original newspaper clipping over two hundred years old! Saying what?"

"I know. I was pretty excited to tell you the truth. And it was in pristine condition—written by one of the French news agencies back then. The word usage was a bit archaic, so I had to call in a favor to get it translated. Anyway, it was a news report on the death of King Louis XVI and Marie Antoinette's son, Louis Charles de France."

"Wait, *the* Marie Antoinette who was beheaded in the French Revolution."

"The one and only."

"I didn't know they had a son."

"I didn't either, but there it was—black on pale yellow complete with a sketch of his face and everything. It said he was only ten years old and that he had died from tuberculosis."

"Okay, so what were you supposed to do with that information?"

"I don't know. The article went on to say that, because of the boy's death, the monarchy had been destroyed, thereby officially declaring France a republic."

"So nothing we don't know already. What's so significant about that? They had a son, and he died. So what? They all died. France was in chaos, and Europe was at war."

"That's what I had thought too, but then I did some research. Several theories claim that, in reality, King Louis XVI and Marie Antoinette were beheaded to bring down the monarchy; that it was some plot against France and not because the people accused him of treason and that she lived a wealthy life while the rest of France starved to death. That was just a smokescreen to keep the people happy. An excuse to execute them. A group of historian theorists all believe that somebody had intentionally killed them off, targeted on purpose with the sole intent of doing away with the monarchy so France could become a republic: liberty, equality, fraternity, all that stuff."

"Yes, and all it meant was that their son inherited the crown after they died. Then he died of TB taking the monarchy with him, and the war carried on. The end and the rest is history."

"I guess that's what everyone thinks happened and maybe it's still true. Heck, until I received this a couple of days ago, I would have agreed."

Alex took a prepaid mobile phone from her bag and opened it up to a photo.

Sam frowned. "Is that what I think it is?"

"I have no idea what it is. I was hoping you'd know," she said, chewing at the dead skin on the side of her thumbnail.

Sam grinned from ear to ear. "Glad to know I'm still useful after that Mission Impossible stuff you pulled on me yesterday. Here I am under the impression that you need my help, meanwhile..."

"Focus, Sam. I can't get into that right now. What are we looking at here?"

Sam moved his fingers across the mobile's screen, zooming in on the photo of a dark brown leather-like object in a glass jar.

"Yep, it looks like a heart to me."

"A heart? As in a human heart? Are you sure?"

"I might have turned archaeologist, but I still have my medical degree, my love. Yes, it's a heart. Fossilized but very much a human heart nonetheless."

Alex slumped into one of the deckchairs and stared out to where the moon's light illuminated the ocean in front of them.

"Was there a message that came with the picture?" Sam asked as he sat down next to her. He could see she was trying her level best to piece the puzzle together.

She shook her head.

"What do you think the heart has to do with the revolution and the boy's death?" Sam interrupted her thoughts.

"I'm not entirely sure. There is some speculation that the boy never died and that no one ever saw his body or knows where they buried him."

"They used to burn the corpses back then—to stop diseases from spreading. That's probably precisely what they did since the lad died of tuberculosis."

"Probably, but I also found out that for decades now several people have stepped forward professing to be descendants of the Dauphin; wanting to claim their inheritance. Of course, that meant that they believed the boy never died and supposedly lived to have children."

"The Dauphin. Was that a pet name?"

"It was the French title given to a future king. You should really brush up on your history."

"I have you to fill in the blanks for me, sweetheart. Bottom line is it might just be another nutcase thinking he's the little guy's offspring and now wants to use you to claim his fortune."

"Then whose heart is inside this glass jar? What is it supposed to mean? What does any of this have to do with my torture, huh? Makes no sense."

The pair silently stared out across the ocean. Each was trying to work out the enigma on their own.

It was Alex who eventually spoke again. "Do you think this heart was the boy's?"

"I'm not sure it would have been possible to keep it so well preserved for over two centuries, but you never know. Perhaps if the person knew what he was doing, but if it is his heart, what would Mr. Anonymous need you for? All it does is prove all these nutcases aren't his descendants and that the history books were right."

Alex turned and faced Sam. Fear lay shallow in her tired eyes. "What if the heart in the jar is meant to be a warning to me? You know, that they'll cut my heart out or something."

"I doubt that's what this is about, Alex."

"Then why was I tortured into submission and shot at? Who broke into my apartment, and why did they tell me not to meddle in their business?"

Sam stared at the ocean and eventually spoke.

"I reckon we should find out; play along with his game and wait for the next clue. See where it goes. "

"Absolutely not Sam! I think we should take it to the police. McDowell seemed reasonable enough to—"

"Not until we know more. We can't trust anyone, not even the police. Besides, what are they going to do? Put us in witness protection? Based on what evidence? I'm not even entirely sure the police can be trusted."

"What? Why not? It's Scotland Yard, Sam, and they don't take on frivolous domestic cases. They must know something we don't."

"There is no case, Alex. It's an inquiry at this stage. Think about it. This Mr. Anonymous helped us escape and managed to get us both here in one piece. He's got something else planned. Maybe another piece in the jigsaw puzzle. Something tells me there's a lot more going on here than we think and he's the key. Going to the police will be a mistake. There was a strange-looking man behind the one-way mirror at my interrogation today, and I'm pretty certain he wasn't an officer of the law—in any country."

"You could see him?"

"In the passage afterward, yes."

"What did he look like?"

"Well dressed, with an antique pewter cane. Black hair, dark eyes, about five eight and the authority to call the shots. The weird thing is I got the feeling he *wanted* me to see his face."

"Did he say anything?"

"No, he didn't have to. His eyes said it all."

"Sorry for bailing on you this morning but I knew you'd be fine. The police had nothing to arrest you for." Alex stifled a yawn and Sam took her in his arms.

"We'll figure it out, okay? We always do. For now, let's get some sleep. Things might be clearer in the morning."

♟

"Where do we go from here?" Alex asked Sam the next morning as she sat peering over the brim of her coffee cup.

"We get something to eat. There's nothing but baked beans in the pantry."

"You're impossible, do you know that? How can you eat at a time like this?"

"I'm just making sure our bodies are fueled and prepared for whatever might come our way today. I can't run away from someone on an empty stomach. Come on, I know this quaint little place down the road that makes the best omelets. Besides, we have no idea how long we'll have to be here before we receive his next instruction."

But when Alex and Sam opened the front door and stepped out another brown envelope lay waiting at their feet.

"You might need to put that jet fuel on ice," Alex commented as she bent to pick it up.

"Wait! What if it's a letter bomb or there's anthrax on it or something?"

"It's not a bomb, silly. Is it?" Alex added suddenly doubtful that Sam might have a valid point.

"Do you want to take the chance?" Sam queried Alex as he reached into the entrance closet for a pair of winter gloves.

"None of the other envelopes posed a threat. It should be fine."

"Well, that was before someone tried to kill us."

Alex held her breath as Sam knelt next to the envelope and cautiously held it up to the sun before sliding the blade of his pocket knife through the fold.

"Ready?"

Alex nodded in reply and watched as Sam pulled the contents from the envelope.

"Seems we might get an early honeymoon, my love. It's two train tickets to Paris."

Alex took the tickets from Sam's hand and ran her eyes over it. "It departs at eleven am—today! That's just under three hours from now."

"We'll make it, just without a decent breakfast. We'll have to grab ourselves some cheese and wine when we get to the city of love, *amour*," Sam said with a twinkle in his eye.

"Have you lost your mind, Sam? We're not getting on this train or anything else for that matter. We have no idea who's been sending these letters much less why. Who sends photos of human organs? It's madness. He could be leading us into a trap to finish off what he started. What if he's one of those crazies who harvest human organs and sells them on the black market or something? We're not going anywhere."

"If he wanted you dead he could've killed you already. The hospital would have been the perfect place, come to think of it. Heck, any of these packages he's been sending you could have killed you. I don't think that's his motive, Alex."

"What happened to you trying to persuade me to take the desk job at ICCRU? All of those 'my job is too dangerous' arguments you've been throwing at me for the last year. It's too risky, Sam. It's suicide!"

Sam folded his arms and turned as if to go back into the cottage. "Yes, you're right. It's too risky. I mean, what was I thinking? That ordinary people like us could potentially debunk an eighteenth-century myth and rewrite history. That's insane. Who cares if they intentionally brought down the monarchy and murdered the future King of France? We should leave it alone."

"Okay I see what you're doing, and that's not fair."

"So it's working? Come on, Alex. You can't tell me you're able to walk away from this. You love history, and besides, you've got me. We can do this. The way I see it, you don't have much choice either. We can't go back to either of our apartments."

Sam waved the two train tickets in the air. "You know you

want to. It's Paris, Alex! The city of love. I'll let you be my private history tutor."

Alex turned her back to Sam and stared out at the ocean waves crashing against the steep rocky cliff below. He was right, of course. Her back was up against a wall with nowhere to turn but trust whoever had been sending these letters.

"We might be traveling to Paris, Sam, but I assure you it won't be red wine and baguettes under the starry night sky. We could be walking straight into a trap for all we know. We're going to need to stay alert and expect the worse."

"So that's a yes?" Sam grinned. "I knew you couldn't resist. Now, perhaps we should seize the moment and get married while we're there."

The stern look in his fiancée's eyes as she walked around the car to open the door said it all and Sam threw his hands in the air. "What? You want to elope, so let's do it. I can't wait to make you my missus. It will take five minutes, ten at the most if we can get an English-speaking official."

"Have you lost your mind, Sam Quinn? And have my new mother-in-law never speak to me again? She's planning the wedding of the century for her only son. She will never let us live that down. I'd rather fight off the bad guys than deal with her wrath. Besides, we have no idea why we're being sent to Paris or even by whom. Let's focus on staying alive so we can have a wedding, okay?"

"Fine, enough with the jokes, promise. Speaking of jokes, I suppose we should put on the ridiculous disguises if we're heading back into London. What did Mr. Anonymous give you to wear?" Sam straightened his mustache in the mirror.

"I think I'm supposed to be Dolly Parton," Alex said amused as she pushed the last strand of her dark brown hair under the blonde wig, turning to take in Sam's disguise.

"That means you must be Kenny Rogers."

Sam stared at his image in the mirror. "You're right. I thought I was Elton John. Well, then islands in the stream we are. At least now we know a bit more about Mr. Anonymous. He can't be that young, and he loves country music."

CHAPTER SIX

S t Pancras station was bustling with railway commuters as Alex and Sam entered. Mesmerized by its beauty, it was hard for them not to stop and admire the impressive Gothic architecture and glass ceiling.

"Do you know this station opened in 1868? It survived World War II, actually," Sam volunteered as their eyes searched the electronic display screen for the train information.

"And you know this how?"

"My grandfather used to tell me stories about it. This entire section here got bombed in 1941. Five bombs penetrated through the platform and the floor to the undercroft and exploded against the sidewall of the tunnel. They had to rebuild it all."

Alex scoured the station, too absorbed to commend Sam on his general knowledge and proceeded through the hall in search of an information kiosk. Trailing behind her, Sam pulled the two tickets from his pocket. "Why do women always want to stop for directions when everything is right here on the ticket? See, platform seven; I think we should take the stairs over there."

Alex didn't answer what she assumed was a rhetorical question in the first place, and the couple cautiously proceeded toward the impressive staircase in the center of the grand booking hall.

"You do of course know we're not exactly blending with the crowd in these ridiculous wigs." Sam spoke softly.

"I know. I think once we're on board, we could take them off. I don't think anyone's following us."

"Great, it makes my head itch."

Halfway up the multitude of steps, she looked back at the ground level. With a birds-eye view, she spotted two well-dressed men in identical taupe suits on opposite ends of the hall — each pretending to read the newspaper.

"Don't look back, they're here," she alerted Sam. "Just act normally."

"How is it they found us? There was no way anyone followed us."

"I don't know, but I don't think they've spotted us yet, Sam. Move over there, toward that group."

A group of tourists stood huddled around their tour leader on the stairs, listening intently to information on the station's history. Alex and Sam blended in amongst them, all the while keeping their eyes on the men down below. When the tour group started moving up the stairs, the pair continued along with them, relieved to have remained undetected.

"This way." Sam ushered Alex along as the group paused for another lecture halfway to the top of the stairs. Now out of the suited men's sight, they moved quickly toward the seventh platform where the train was already waiting. As they slipped on board between the glass doors, they heard angered cries coming from the tour group on the platform behind them. Alex looked back through the train's windows and watched as the suited men hurriedly made their way to the top of the stairs, leaving a bunch of upset tourists in their wake.

"In here," Sam called out and pulled Alex into the semi-private two-seater berth allocated to their tickets. "Where's a closed compartment when you need one?" he muttered under his breath.

"I don't think they're alone, Sam. I'm certain they couldn't have spotted us from the ground floor. Not with these disguises on and hiding between the tour members," Alex commented.

"I'd agree with you. Let's hope, however many thugs there

are, they didn't see us board this train. It's not like there's anywhere to hide in here."

Sam drew the blinds down over the windows and popped his head around the seating just enough to get a visual of the narrow corridor.

"So far, it's clear. I can't see anyone."

"We leave in one minute. If these guys are smart, which I think they are, they will put two and two together. Right now this is the only train to Paris, and well, since it's all about French history, this seems the obvious choice. We can only hope they don't make it on in time."

Sam pulled off his wig and mustache. "Well, one thing's for sure, I've had enough of Kenny Rogers. Dolly is welcome to stay, but Kenny dies here. Besides, if they did see us, they'd be looking out for them, not us."

Alex smiled and pulled her blonde wig off too. "You're right. Chances are they already spotted Dolly and Kenny. Here, pop this on." She pulled two black peak caps from her backpack before reaching for the gun in her waistband. Obscured from the view of passers-by she held the gun under the small table in front of her and dropped the magazine into her hand, briefly checking it before clicking it back into place.

"Who do you suppose they are?" she asked Sam who prepared his gun too.

"I haven't the foggiest, Alex, but one thing's for sure. If Scotland Yard is involved, there's a lot more brewing here. The officer at the police station told me they arrested two of the shooters and that they had links to open Interpol cases. Her file was labeled 'top secret'. You've opened a can of worms if you ask me."

"What makes you think I opened anything? The letters came to me, remember. It wasn't by choice."

Sam leaned across the table. "The way I see it we have one way out of this and that's to find Mr. Anonymous before these guys catch us. He's the one leading us on this wild goose chase after something we're not even sure of what."

Alex nodded in agreement just as the train started moving.

"Think they made it on?"

"Don't know," Sam answered and sneaked another look down the corridor. Relieved there was no one but a rowdy group of young men still settling into their seats, he rested his head against the headrest and exhaled. "I think we escaped them."

"I wouldn't get too settled, Sam. They'll have us cornered once we start moving. It's not as if we can jump off a train moving at a hundred and fifty miles per hour."

"What are we supposed to do once we reach Paris?"

Still contemplating her answer, Alex spotted the two suited

men pushing their way from the adjoining carriage toward them.

"We have company, Sam. They're coming up behind you, let's go!" Alex said as she bolted from her seat in the opposite direction toward the party-spirited group of men at the end of their carriage. Their sudden departure alerted their stalkers who hurriedly set out after them. Alex squeezed her way through the noisy bachelor party that was spilling over into the narrow walkthrough, and one of them grabbed her bottom. With no time to handle the immature alpha males, she ignored it. Behind her, Sam squeezed through the already tipsy rumbustious group — his knee voluntarily colliding with the fellow's groin.

"Watch it, you fool!" The young man bellowed, folding over in pain.

Sam giggled under his breath as Alex and he slipped through the dividing doors into the next carriage, leaving the suits to fight their way through the unimpressed bachelor party.

With nowhere to go but forward the pair swiftly navigated their way through the next coach which was far more occupied than the previous one. The tourists from the stairs were pinned down by another history lesson, some of them blocking the narrow aisle as they stood closer to their guide.

"Sorry, excuse me... coming through," Alex politely

pleaded her way between two chatty amply-proportioned women who stood firmly planted in the middle of the aisle.

"Thank you, ladies. Sorry for the disturbance," Sam added as he too squeezed his way through.

Whatever time they lost with the chubby sisters they managed to make up as they ran down the aisle of the next carriage which luckily was unobstructed. A full two hours travel time remained, and the front of the train loomed closer.

"In here," Alex ducked into the washrooms at the end of the next carriage pulling Sam in with her. "We'll wait for them to pass us and then slip out and head off toward the rear of the train."

"So, what then? We keep running back and forth through the train for two hours?" Sam whispered, leaning his ear against the shiny steel door.

"I'm open to suggestions. We're trapped in here, remember?"

Sam held his index finger up against his mouth as he heard the men's feet hit the steel floor outside the door. Alex cocked her gun and pointed it toward the floor, both hands firmly on the grip and ready to shoot. The partition door to the next car opened and closed, followed by silence.

"They're gone. Ready?" Sam whispered with his hand steady on the door latch.

Alex nodded, briefly flexing her fingers around her gun's

grip before tightening her hold. Sam flipped the cubicle's latch off and slowly pulled the door open toward him. Without warning the door thrust against his chest and he fell back into Alex, pinning her against the washbasin behind them and sending her gun to the floor. The surprise attack left them both scrambling to gain control, but the hard blow of a man's fist against his cheekbone made Sam fall back against Alex again, slamming her head hard against the protruding plumbing on the wall behind them. Sam fought back, blocking another incoming punch with his forearm. Finally, on his feet and off Alex, he pushed his attacker out into the open space in front of the washroom. His knee rammed hard into the suited man's side. The man attempted another underarm hook into Sam's abdomen, but again Sam blocked it. Sam delivered a forceful right hook across the man's left eye, making him stumble off balance back into the cubicle.

On cue, Alex drove her foot into the area behind their attacker's knee, bringing him to the ground in front of Sam's feet. Sam slammed his elbow hard into the nape of the guy's neck, but the man fought back and rammed his fist into Sam's groin, leaving him breathless. At that moment, Alex felt a cable come around her neck from the doorway behind her, instantly blocking off her windpipe. She reached both hands back into the second attacker's face and drove her fingernails into his flesh. The man tightened the cable around her neck, forcing her to let go. Unable to breathe, she felt the air being squeezed from her body, momentarily leaving her disorientated. In front of her, she watched as the first attacker pushed Sam's face down onto the floor, strangling him with a thin black cord. Desperate to alleviate the pressure on her throat, she tried forcing two of her fingers between the cable and her flesh but soon gave up realizing it was impossible.

She pushed her feet firmly against the doorframe and propelled her attacker backward, slamming him hard against the wall behind them. It did nothing other than releasing the cord around her neck just enough to allow the tiniest bit of air to flow into her lungs. Her attacker recovered fast and immediately set about tightening the cable around her throat again. But she stomped her heel firmly onto her assailant's foot and thrust her elbow back between his ribs, forcing him to let go of the cable. Alex flicked her head back and into her attacker's nose, leaving him with a bleeding broken nose. With her attacker now somewhat immobile on the floor behind her, she turned her attention back to where Sam was still fighting for his life inside the washroom.

Alex extended her arms over her head and took hold of the steel plumbing that ran across the wall above the toilet door. She hoisted her body up and delivered a powerful kick against the attacker's cheek. He stumbled back, letting go of the cord around Sam's neck. The guy with the broken nose surprised her from behind and tried to slip the tie around her throat again. Quick on her feet, Alex leaned in and used his body as leverage instead to twist both her ankles around the neck of Sam's attacker, choking him until he fell unconscious to the floor. She jerked her head back and broke her attacker's nose for a second time. Still trying to recover, Sam drove his fist into the guy's left kidney and followed on with a left hook to his jawbone.

The blow finally rendered him unconscious next to his associate on the floor.

CHAPTER SEVEN

"You okay?" Sam asked as he rubbed his throat and fell back, exhausted against the doorframe.

"Think so, you?"

"I'll live. The scumbag left you with a bleeding lip though. We should get some ice on that."

Sam touched the corner of her cracked lip with his thumb. "But boy did you teach them a lesson. It looks like you might have sneaked in a few more training sessions behind my back."

"Yeah well, glad it paid off. It could've easily gone wrong, you know. We should tie these guys up before they wake up. You take his feet."

They dragged the two men next to each other into the small washroom and sat them back to back on the floor.

"Thanks for the cord, fellows," Sam gloated as he criss-crossed it firmly around both their hands and feet.

"Wait! We should check their pockets. Maybe we'll be lucky enough to find out who they are."

Alex slipped her hands into the pockets of the first guy's jacket while Sam checked his pants.

"No wallet or ID here," Sam said as he started his search of the next man which also turned up empty.

"One would think they'd have a mobile at least," he added.

"That's strange, why do you think he walks around with this in his pocket?" Alex asked when she pulled out a solid brass chess piece from the first attacker's breast pocket.

"It's a pawn from a chess set. Maybe a lucky charm or something?" Sam ventured.

"I don't think so. Look, this guy has one too."

"That is strange. What are the odds they both have the same lucky charms? They're identical. Unless of course they play chess during their lunch breaks."

"You're funny. I don't think these guys take lunch breaks, Sam."

Alex inspected the two solid brass chess pawns in her hands before slipping them into the small pocket of her denim jeans.

"No time to figure it out now. Let's wrap it up with these two before someone finds us."

Sam broke off the door handle and the lock to secure them inside the washroom. "There, that should do it; no way these two can escape. Let's grab some lunch. I'm starving."

"You never did have your breakfast," Alex laughed, flinching when her lip stung from her injury.

The dining car was full of life and energy with the tour group taking up most of the tables, and Alex and Sam took a seat at the small bistro bar at the other end of the carriage.

"Give us a scotch, please mate. It's five o'clock some-where," Sam ordered from the barman, feeling like he needed more than a coffee, "and one for my fiancée too, please? She might actually need it more than me."

He wrapped a few blocks of ice from a nearby ice bucket in his napkin and stuck it in Alex's hand.

"You know what we're doing here is pure insanity, don't you? Those guys back there could have killed us. And for what?" Sam said as he threw back his whiskey.

"You're the one who insisted we should get on this train, remember?"

"I know, but I'm starting to regret it now. You were right,

Alex. This is insane. We've been on many missions together, but this one? This one is suicide. We're out here on a whim following bread crumbs dropped by some nutcase, with no idea who he is or what we're supposed to find at the end of this little game of his. Not to mention the fact that we're being hunted down by heaven knows who? So here we are, stuck in the middle between two evils, neither of which we have knowledge of, and we're playing along? You were right. That does sound insane."

"What makes you think Mr. Anonymous is evil? If anything, it seems he's been keeping us safe."

"Safe! Alex, the guy got us onto this train in the first place. Who's to say those two in the bathroom don't work for him? How did they know we were here? What if you're right and it was a trap? What if he is the one trying to kill us?"

"Well, glad you finally see things my way, but why would he want to kill us? His note said he needed my help. I fail to see a motive here. And whose business did I get warned to stay out of?"

"We should call this off and go to the police."

"No, I don't think the two are connected, Sam. Something's up, and I'm going to find out what."

"So you're going to blindly chase after something and ignore the fact that they warned you not to meddle in their business? You have no idea what or who you're involved with, Alex. Your life, heck both our lives are now at stake here!"

Alex flipped the menu open and started scanning through the meal options.

"Sweetheart, ignoring me isn't going to make this go away." Sam took hold of her hands and turned her to face him. "I can't lose you, Alex. Truth is, I'm scared for both of us."

Sam was right to be scared. She knew the entire mission was foolish, but something inside her couldn't let go now until she knew the truth. Discovering the two brass pawns had her more curious now than ever before.

"I know, Sam. I'm sorry I got you into this, but I can't back off now. You said it yourself. How do we turn away from something that might lead to the greatest exposé in history? What if that newspaper article leads us to the dauphin's remains? Or better yet, what if we discover there really wasn't a body in the first place and that he never died? We'd solve a historical mystery that's been plaguing people all around the world for centuries. What if all this unlocks facts surrounding the French Revolution? The French Revolution, Sam! Do you know how big that is?"

Sam watched as Alex's eyes lit up with excitement. He'd fallen in love with her the moment he first saw that precise passion for archaeology back in Tanzania. What's more, was that Sam couldn't deny that the prospect excited him too. He looked down at the ring on her left hand and flicked his thumb over the one-carat tanzanite stone.

"When I asked your father for your hand in marriage, he told me something. He said I should never try to clip your wings and that you were always meant to discover a great many things." He gazed into her eyes. "You're the most remarkable woman I know, Alex, and when I put this ring on your finger, it was for life. One day, I'm hoping we could start a family, and when that time comes, we'll take the safe road. But for now, I'm with you, no matter what and no matter where it takes you. But promise me one thing, we stick together, and you never keep anything from me again, okay?"

Alex nodded and whispered, "Promise," her heart bursting with love for Sam.

"Great, now can we please eat before I pass out?"

The rest of the train ride into Paris bore no danger, and Alex and Sam stepped out onto the platform at the Gare du Nord terminus in the center of Paris.

"I thought St Pancras was busy. This place is buzzing. Now what?" Sam paused, looking out into the crowded station.

"I don't know. I guess we find a hotel for the night and hope

Mr. Anonymous communicates with us in due course. He always seems to know where to find us."

"Spot any surprise welcome parties?" Sam asked as they scanned the terminal for any suspicious-looking men in taupe suits.

"Looks clear to me."

"Pardon, mademoiselle, you forgot your purse." A friendly Frenchman called out from the platform behind them, waving a crossbody clutch handbag in the air.

"Oh no-no, it's not mine," Alex responded, holding up her hand.

"Oui oui, it is yours. You left it at the bar," the man insisted and shoved it in her hands before disappearing down the nearby escalator.

Alex stared at the black embellished handbag in her hand. A pink beaded poodle next to a sequined picture of the Eiffel tower stared back at her; the words Ooh-La-La written in white chalk-like font across the top.

"And that's how you know you're in Paris," Sam joked. "Well, open it. Something tells me it's another one of Mr. Anonymous' special deliveries."

Alex didn't hesitate and flipped the pink silk-lined flap open to reveal a gold embossed card and a digital key to a hotel.

"It's an invitation," she said, declaring the obvious to Sam before reading it out loud.

Your presence is requested at the annual
Le Grand Bal Masqué
du Château de Versailles

"A masked ball. Sounds like my kind of party," Sam said excitedly. "When is it?"

"Tonight."

"Well, then, mademoiselle, we should find the hotel and hope they can help us find some costumes to wear. I don't think Kenny and Dollie will quite suit this particular affair. Where do you suppose we can find a taxi?"

♟

The hotel was a lavishly appointed five-star establishment in the center of Paris. It was hard not to get caught up in the grand ambiance it evoked. With her nerves now slightly less on edge, it didn't take Alex long to settle in. Her over-the-top suite offered a spectacular view from her balcony, enjoying the full splendor of the magnificent view of the Paris skyline. In the adjoining suite, Sam took full advantage of the caviar platter and steam shower, feeling and acting every bit like a king. That being so, it also came as no surprise that their baroque costumes for the masked ball were ready and waiting for them in their wardrobes.

Alex had never been to a masked ball before. It wasn't entirely her scene, but when she faced the mirror and caught full sight of her dress, French royalty flooded her senses. Traveling the world with her explorer parents, cargo pants and T-shirts had always been her garments of choice. She had never been one for black satin and lace. But now, staring at her image in the mirror from beneath the black lace mask covering half her face, she found herself liking it more than she ever thought possible.

"Wow! Who are you, and what have you done with my fiancée?"

Sam sneaked up behind her.

"You look like you might actually be a queen. Aren't I a lucky man?"

"One night only, Sam Quinn," Alex replied, feeling embarrassed for getting caught admiring herself.

"I hear there is a chapel in the palace. Sure you don't want to tie the knot tonight?" Sam whispered against her neck.

"I'm sure. Perhaps you might need to take a cold shower before we go."

"That's a shame," he said, ignoring her naughty comment, "Paris could be something you'd never forget."

Alex giggled. "Behave yourself. We have business matters to take care of." She reached for her gun and slipped it into a holster strapped to her thigh underneath her dress.

A brief knock at the door announced the arrival of a hotel attendant.

"Ah the life of the wealthy, never a private moment when you need one."

"You do know we're not actually wealthy, right? All this is make-believe," Alex reminded him.

"All in the name of business, yes," Sam called back as he invited the attendant in.

"Your car is waiting, monsieur, mademoiselle," the staffer announced before leaving as quickly as he'd appeared.

"Well, you heard the man. Let's get this party started. Shall we go then, my queen? Apparently, we now also have a car waiting for us downstairs. You really know how to pick them, that's certain. I don't think I've ever stayed in a hotel this fancy. I feel like we won the lottery."

CHAPTER EIGHT

W hen they reached the hotel foyer, they were greeted by their now-familiar room attendant who discreetly ushered them into a dark alley from the rear exit of the hotel and then promptly turned and closed the door behind them.

"Please follow me, monsieur, mademoiselle."

A male voice suddenly spoke behind them, and Alex and Sam swung around to meet a tall man wearing a black suit and tie and black leather gloves.

A reflex reaction had Alex reach for her gun but she stopped when the man spoke again.

"No need, mademoiselle, I mean you no harm. Just following orders."

"Whose orders? Who sent you?" Sam questioned.

"My master will reveal himself soon. Please, follow me to the car. I will be your driver to the Château de Versailles."

"*My master?*" Sam whispered to Alex as they followed the man through the empty alley around the back of the hotel to where a shiny white car was parked.

"Oh, this guy has money, lots of it too if you ask me," Sam said, bursting with excitement as they set eyes on the luxury vehicle.

"I can definitely get used to this," Sam added when they slipped into the red leather seats.

"I wouldn't get too carried away if I were you. Cinderella's coach turned back into a pumpkin at midnight. Let's not forget why we're here." Alex was cautiously keeping her eye on the driver as he walked around to get into the car.

"Don't be such a party pooper, Alex. When have you ever been driven around Paris in a car like this? It's a Rolls Royce Phantom for crying out loud. Not to mention attending a masked ball in a real palace. Live a little, my love. This could be our pre-wedding honeymoon. We could still elope, you know. I'm sure our driver knows a clergy who can marry us at short notice."

The chauffeur slipped in behind the wheel and promptly suggested that they pour themselves a glass of the special reserve Dom Perignon that lay snug in an ice bucket behind a small compartment.

"Don't mind if I do, thank you…" Sam paused, hinting for the driver to introduce himself.

"Philippe, sir."

"Well, Philippe, nice to meet you."

"Who is this *master* you speak of? Who do you work for, Philippe?" Alex interrupted the pleasantries. But the driver merely responded by closing the window partitioning between them.

"Here, have a glass of proper champagne. You might as well sit back and enjoy the evening, Alex. You're not going to get anything out of this guy. He's loyal to a fault. Probably gets paid enough to keep his mouth shut. Obviously Mr. Anonymous needs to keep us sweet and if this is what that translates to, I'm all in."

"I mean it, Sam. Don't get too comfortable. All this is smoke and mirrors. Might I remind you that we have no idea who this man is or what he wants from us? We need to stay focused. One slip and we could end up dead."

Sam popped the champagne back into the ice bucket and cleared his throat.

"You're right, Alex. We shouldn't touch the thousand-pound French champagne and go to, what I assume would be an invitation-only masked ball at a real French palace. So what if this is a once in a lifetime experience? To live like the rich and famous for one night, only to be killed by our host. We should not enjoy any of this and expect the worse."

Alex shot Sam a stern look, annoyed at his sarcastic reply. But, as desperate as she was to be angered by his derisive mocking, the playful twinkle in his eyes melted all her defenses. He was right. It's not every day they were treated like royalty.

"Okay fine, I suppose you're right. I doubt the man would be spending this much money wining and dining us if he wanted to kill us."

"Precisely, now sit back and enjoy the experience. Sometimes you need to have a little trust in people. Not everyone is a bad guy. We'll be fine. Here's to a night of living it up in Paris. Vive la France!"

As the couple stepped out of their chauffeur-driven car inside the opulent gates of the Palace of Versailles, a majestic aura lay thick in the air. Dozens of people dressed in similar baroque garb lined the pristine landscaped garden paths around an enormous center fountain. Topiary trees and perfectly pruned shrubs announced the fact that they were walking where a proper King and Queen of France once strolled. But inside the walls of the chateau, it wasn't at all the formal affair they had expected to see. Colorful lasers beamed over their heads while loud modern party music had encouraged several small groups to dance. Entertainers performed on a stage under brightly colored flashing disco lights, and trapeze artists swung from overhead scaffolds, making it seem more reminiscent of a young people's club scene than a royal ball.

"Okay, so this is a little different from what I thought it would be, but it will do. Let's mingle," Sam said playfully.

"No, monsieur, you're expected in the Salon d'Hercule," Philippe beckoned.

"Salon d'what?" Sam asked.

"Salon d'Hercule, monsieur. It was the king and queen's drawing room where the main suppers, balls and receptions were held," Philippe informed them.

"So it's a private party separate from all of this?"

"Oui, mademoiselle."

Intrigued, Alex and Sam followed Philippe as he led them through a doorway to a gallery that extended more than two hundred feet. The walls were decorated with a dozen or more wide arcaded mirrors each opposite a large window that overlooked the gardens below. Glass chandeliers adorned the arched, ornately painted ceiling upon which a series of scenes depicted the glorious history of Louis XIV. The vaulted ceilings were encrusted with what seemed like pure gold. Beams of light glistened in a kaleidoscope off of the gold decals and gilded statues that bordered the marble walls. Large arched windows, each with a gilded pillar and separate chandeliers, forced its visitors' attention to the spectacular views over Paris.

"I guess this is where Trump took his inspiration from. I don't think I've ever seen more gold adorn any walls and ceilings than this," Sam joked. "I mean, look at these views!"

"Isn't it spectacular? Can you imagine living here? Such opulence. No wonder it angered the Parisians. The monarchy lived like this while they barely had bread to eat."

Philippe stopped when they reached the other side of the room and opened the glass-paned French doors. "Follow the stairs and enter to your right. Enjoy your evening."

"That's it? You're not staying?" Sam teased only to receive a barely noticeable smile from Philippe before he turned and left.

"Do you think we're going to meet Mr. Anonymous?" Alex whispered to Sam.

"Now that would be nice. We can put an end to this silly game of his."

But much to their disappointment their arrival in the even more luxurious ballroom was met by about four dozen guests distinctly higher in class than the partying crowd they had just left. So too was the ambiance the exact opposite than when they'd arrived with soft classical music playing in the background and small cliques of men and women in subdued discussion.

"And there it is, the rude awakening that we're not wealthy. I feel like a fish out of water," Sam whispered.

"We should move around, blend in," Alex whispered back, grateful the mask hid her discomfort.

"Why do you think Mr. Anonymous brought us here? To feel what it was like to live amongst the noblemen in the royal castle?" Sam asked.

"Not sure, but judging from the two at your ten o'clock, I'd think we had better take it easy on the champagne."

Sam's eyes trailed to the two men Alex pointed out and then landed on two more to the right of them. "They're not alone. Might just be that trap we were talking about. Think it's the guys from the train?"

"Hard to say with the masks on. Stay off the bubbly, Sam. For all we know they laced it."

While they slowly moved through the crowded space a couple who looked considerably less stuck-up than the rest motioned for them to come closer.

"Good evening, may we join you?" Alex asked with her limited French vocabulary.

"Oui, but of course," a tall, burly Frenchman with a big

nose and almost bearlike demeanor answered; his perfect English only slightly laced with a French accent.

"Forgive me; I haven't spoken French since my school years."

"No need to apologize, madame. There are quite a few of us who speak perfect English. We're all here for the same reason, no?"

"Indeed," Sam interrupted, "wouldn't miss something this exciting."

"Well, exciting isn't quite how we'd describe it in French, but I suppose you have a different meaning for the word in English," he said, pushing out his big belly as he proudly threw his shoulders back.

Alex shuffled uncomfortably in the wake of their overt declaration that they didn't have the slightest notion why their guests were there. "How would you describe it, monsieur? Perhaps you'd be so kind as to give us a lesson in your fine language."

"But of course, madame. With something as sacred as this only happening once a year, it would not be right of me not to honor the Royal Family. We have indeed suffered a great loss."

"Sacred indeed, yes," she echoed in the hopes of baiting him for more information when the bubbly French woman behind him interrupted.

"Aren't you going to introduce us, Etiénne?"

"You're right, *mon chérie*, we have not introduced ourselves. Forgive my rudeness. I am Count Etiénne du Bois, and this is my beautiful wife, Josephine."

"Nice to meet you, I'm..." Alex paused, briefly contemplating whether she should divulge their real names and then continued, "Elizabeth and this is James."

Relieved Alex had the swiftness of mind, Sam played along, and, with authentic French charm, kissed the back of Josephine's hand.

"You're a lucky woman, Elizabeth. How long have you been married?"

"We haven't yet, we're still engaged."

"How lovely?" She batted her eyes at Sam.

"When is the wedding?" Josephine continued her inquest.

"In a couple of weeks," Alex smiled.

"You can't go wrong with a French wedding. The lavender is in full bloom this time of year."

"That's precisely what I said, Josephine. No one does 'love' quite like the French right?" Sam added with that all too familiar twinkle in his eye.

The music suddenly stopped and, as if one body, everyone turned and faced the front of the room.

A distinguished gentleman wearing a gold embroidered three-quarter length jacket, and peacock blue sash entered the back of the room and passed through a line of six similarly dressed men. Looking like he'd just stepped out of the history books he took his place behind the small podium.

"Who's that?" Sam whispered to Josephine, who stood far too close to him.

"That's Lord Alphonse. We have him to thank for this lavish affair."

The room listened as the French-speaking lord welcomed everyone before reading from what appeared to be an ancient scroll.

"My French is a tad rusty; what's he reading?" Sam whispered to Alex.

"Something about a life cut short and the memory of the monarchy. It sounds a bit like a eulogy," Alex replied.

Lord Alphonse continued reading from the scroll for another fifteen minutes after which he then lit ten candles while a priest prayed. Acutely aware of still being watched, Alex didn't close her eyes. Instead, she took the opportunity to scan over the guests. When the prayer finally ended a blue and gold satin pillow was passed down the line of men who all wore matching blue jackets with white sashes. The guests responded by crossing themselves as Roman Catholics typically did in a blessing.

"I feel like this is a church service. What's happening?" It was Alex who asked Sam this time to which he just shrugged his shoulders.

One of the blue jackets moved between the guests carrying the blue and gold pillow to which several guests responded with the same French saying. Alex and Sam waited for the pillow to come past, eager to see what was on top. And when it did, it merely displayed three gold embroidered letters: L.C.B

"What's LCB?" Sam asked Josephine after the pillow made its way back to the front of the hall.

"My dear, James, you do not know? Louis Charles Bourbon of course. That's why we're here, silly; to remember the sweet boy. He died so frightfully young. That was the young prince's pillow before they took him, poor thing."

Josephine fanned herself as if she was about to faint. Alex and Sam exchanged looks as they came to realize it was a memorial for the dauphin.

"You really think he died of tuberculosis?" Sam quietly nudged Josephine for answers, purposefully standing closer to her. She liked him, and he used it to glean the information they desperately needed.

"But of course, James. It was written in the history books, no?"

"That doesn't mean it's true, *mon chérie,*" the count whispered before continuing. "We have been debating this for years. My dear Josephine believes he died in that tower. But not I. My *pappy* told me many stories when I was just a young boy and his *pappy* before that."

"So you think the boy never died? That he lived?" Alex whispered back as a small choir filled the room with a somber song.

"I do, Elizabeth. It is said his body was never seen. The doctor was the only one there; declared him dead, but no one saw his body removed from his cell. Many have come looking for his grave over the years, and it's not where the doctor said it was."

"Etiénne, you're filling our new friends' heads with your family's silly stories. Don't listen to him, darlings. They performed an autopsy on the boy. He never lived. All these theories are desperate straws created by royalists like my dear husband over here. If our young dauphin were alive, he would have come back to claim his position as heir, and he never did."

"That cannot be true, *mon chérie*. Lord Alphonse is his royal descendant. How could that happen if the boy died?"

"Pfuh, Lord Alphonse. Darling, Etiénne, Lord Alphonse is nothing but a treasure seeker. The monarchy is dead, and so is the boy."

CHAPTER NINE

While the choir's hymns paid tribute to the young heir who never became king, the count and his bubbly, outspoken wife's political quibble entertained Alex and Sam. And the more they heard, the clearer it became that the exclusive gathering was, in fact, a group of royalists who clung to a monarchy that no longer existed, desperate to believe that Lord Alphonse's claim to be a royal descendent was valid.

"So why are you here, Josephine? I mean if you don't believe he lived," Sam queried.

"My dear, there are two groups of people here, all still believing in the monarchy. We just don't all agree on what happened back then. Some here, like my husband, believe the boy somehow escaped and was adopted, just like his older sister, Marie Thérèse. And the others, like me, believe he died. No one really knows what happened. Many have lent their ears out to ridiculous tales their grandparents made up—unproven tales and gossip." She cleared her throat hinting at her husband being one of them, "but either way, we're all here to remember the young prince and what he went through. Besides, who'd want to miss this? It's the one time of the year we get to debate openly with each other."

"Not to mention my *chèrie* gets a chance to pick up on all the latest gossip," Etiénne teased as he pulled her closer to him and continued their playful banter.

"Sam, your three o'clock," Alex whispered as she marked one of the suspicious-looking men moving along the side of the room toward them.

"I see him. Where are the others?"

Alex scanned the room. "I lost them. We should get out of here."

"Too late. Over there, at the entrance."

"Can you see another way out of here?"

"Nope… unless…"

"What? Unless what, Sam?" Alex whispered back feeling a slight wave of panic rise up.

"Friends, what do you say we all get out of here before you two kill each other? Perhaps you might know how we can do so undetected and without offending our host?" Sam whispered to the quarreling French couple who instantly stopped midway in their now fiery debate.

"Well, James, I think you're right. My husband could do with some cooling off," said Josephine, winking at her red-faced husband who responded simply by shrugging his shoulders in typical French fashion while blowing a puff of air through pursed lips.

"Oui-oui, I know just how," the count responded, somewhat relieved to have escaped the imminent spectacle that seemed to have become their hallmark at these gatherings.

"This way," the count whispered as he quietly led them to the back of the room. From behind the guests where they stood eyes-closed and with their backs toward them in yet another prayer ceremony, he paused, pinning his back against the wall.

"The door is that way," Alex whispered when they lined up against the wall next to him. The count wedged one finger under his big nose over his lips before his hand slipped behind his back against the baroque painted wall behind them. The faintest clicking sound alerted Alex and Sam that the innocent looking Frenchman had somehow opened a secret door behind the paneled wall.

"Well, what do you know?" Sam whispered. "Seems this guy has a few aces up his sleeve."

One by one they managed to slip undetected through the small opening in the wall and descended a narrow, spiral staircase built entirely from stone. With the wall panel securely back in place, the steep staircase disappeared into the darkness, challenging the four escapees to feel their way along the cold walls. Alex yanked off her mask in an attempt to see better in the near pitch-black darkness, but it had little to no effect on her vision—or lack thereof. The air was thin, saturated in a strong musky scent, and icy cold which caused her skin to break out in goosebumps as the chilly air brushed over her bare shoulders.

"Where are we going?" Alex whispered.

"Oh, no need to whisper, my dear," Etiénne chuckled. "These walls are as thick as they come. No one will hear you from down here. It was the very tunnel our Sun King used to visit with his mistresses."

"I literally have no idea who you're talking about, Etiénne," Sam's voice echoed from the back followed by several subdued noises as he continually bumped his head on the low roof of the spiraling steps above his head. "I'm assuming he was the shortest king alive though."

"*Oh, mon Dieu!* You need to study your French history, my friend. King Louis XIV, of course. He called himself the Sun King because he believed in a centralized government with himself at its center. He chose the sun as his emblem; to show off his power to the people. Some say he was a Greek god, like Apollo. It is he who ordered the construction of the Palace of Versailles and that enormous fountain of Apollo in the gardens. He wanted to separate himself from the people. He had many, many mistresses, and this is how he sneaked them into the palace."

"And how is it you know about these secret passages?" Alex asked with curiosity.

"It is not a secret anymore, my friends. These tunnels were discovered in the mid-1800s when they restored the palace, and my great *pappy* was lucky enough to have been part of the restoration team."

"And that's why my beloved husband thinks he knows everything about the Royal Family," Josephine giggled as they finally reached the bottom of the stairs.

"Wait here," Etiénne ordered, and they heard his feet shuffle away from them. Moments later, the welcoming light of a small lantern declared their surroundings.

"What is this place?" Alex asked in awe.

"King Louis XIV's private wine cellar. This is where he used to court his mistresses, here, at this very table," he said ushering them over to a small round wooden table in the center of the damp cellar. Cobwebs clung to the silver candelabra that still held a pair of melted down candles. To the right of the table, a narrow wooden shelf displayed two pewter wine goblets, and a glass carafe also covered in cobwebs.

"This is amazing, Etiénne! Are you telling me this is as it was left when he was here?"

Etiénne shrugged his shoulders again, "Oui-oui, my dear. It was discovered during the renovations and precisely left as it was then, but no one ever recorded it when it was discovered. It's never been open to the public. Now, not many people know it even exists. Most have already passed on and taken it with them to the grave. I only know because my great *pappy* learned it from his father and passed it on through my family. Maybe now my dear Josephine will believe me."

"Still doesn't prove our little dauphin lived," Josephine sneered.

Alex circled the closed-off room looking for a door. "Is there any other way out?"

Etiénne's large clumsy body rapidly moved closer to her. "But of course, dear Elizabeth. It's one of the many secrets I know." He raised his eyebrow at his wife who responded by rolling her eyes and folding her arms across her busty chest.

They watched as Etiénne twisted a sequence of dusty wine bottles, one by one as if turning a combination lock on a safe. Some to the left and others to the right; each time it sounded a soft clicking noise. Twelve turns later and a cloud of dust puffed into the air when one of the wine racks receded into the wall and revealed a small arched opening.

"Ha-ha! I wasn't sure it would still work. The last time I was in here was with my *pappy* when I was a child. It was the best day of my life. Come, come."

Sam squeezed Alex's arm as he watched her face light up. She was especially susceptible to hidden passages and secret doorways. It excited her beyond measure, and Sam loved seeing her come to life like this.

"It's a lot smaller than I remember," Etiénne uttered as he was forced to tip his head onto his shoulder and shuffle sideways to fit through the narrow passage. "Watch your head, James. I have a feeling you might encounter the same challenge as me. Not far now though," he continued with a giggle as his wife squealed each time a spiderweb got tangled in her white wig.

"How deep are we under the ground?" Sam said with the slightest hint of claustrophobia in his voice.

"Deep enough not to want to have all of this cave in on us," Etiénne chuckled, purposefully attempting to evoke a reaction from his wife to drive his point home, but much to his dismay she didn't take the bait. She was too caught up in pulling more webs from her mouth.

The lantern's flame flickered against the grey stone walls followed by the slightest waft of cold air that brushed over their skins.

"Are we close to an exit?" Alex asked.

"Not just yet, my dear. That might have just been a spirit passing through," the count responded.

"A spirit? What do you mean a spirit, Etiénne? I'm not

walking with ghosts. Get me out of here you foolish old man!" Josephine's panicked voice finally spoke.

"Oh yes, *mon chérie*, there are lots of tales about spirits haunting the secret tunnels under the palace. It's said that many of the king's courtiers were killed to conceal his scandalous affairs. They roam the corridors and haunt those who don't respect the monarchy."

"If I die down here, Etiénne Du Bois I will haunt you till the day you die!" Josephine yelled in panic at her mocking husband—her idle threat, causing him to burst into laughter.

"He's joking, Josephine. Ghosts don't exist," Sam comforted her.

A minute later and the narrow, grey-walled passage suddenly opened to a chimney reaching several feet into the darkness above their heads. The faint light of the lantern exposed the rungs of a ladder protruding from the wall that extended upwards into the chimney.

"I'll go first. It's about fifty steps to the top if I remember."

"Hurry on up then, Etiénne, and get us out of here," Josephine urged her husband who further relished her angst as he blew out the lantern's flame and hung it on the wall, casting the small group into total darkness. The sound of his shoes on the rungs echoed through the small space. Alex and Sam counted the steps out with Josephine, trying hard not to giggle at her gullibility.

Fifty-six steps later, they heard the grinding noise of metal against metal before a cloud of dust followed by a heap of pebble-filled sand funneled down the chimney onto their faces.

"Come on then. The coast is clear," the count's whispered voice echoed down toward them, and the trio spotted the starry night sky behind Etiénne's silhouetted head.

It wasn't long before Alex, Sam, and an annoyed Josephine joined their expedition leader in the middle of a landscaped garden maze in the fresh Paris night air.

"You're really pushing my buttons tonight, Etiénne. What's this?" Josephine scowled.

"Well, it's a maze of course *mon chérie*. Isn't it romantic?"

Josephine stomped into one of the paths in search of the exit, mumbling obscene French words under her breath.

"This way, *mon chérie,* I'd hate to see you hit a dead end," the count chuckled, to which his wife made a short, low clucking sound with her tongue and rushed with heavy steps past him.

"I would ease up on her if I were you, Etiénne," Sam said playfully before adding, "you might sleep on the couch tonight."

"That's where you two young ones have it wrong, my friend. This is how true Frenchmen make love. This playful banter will turn into French passion in no time. She'll never admit it, but that old wife of mine loves it. We'll be married forty years this coming spring, and I can tell you from experience, I have her right where I want her."

Amused by their new-found friend's entertaining display of affection, Alex and Sam followed the French couple through the maze to where it finally opened in the expansive gardens of Versailles.

"And *voila!*" the count declared triumphantly, grabbing his wife around her waist and nuzzling his face in her neck. Much to Alex and Sam's surprise, it seemed Etiénne was indeed accurate as they watched how Josephine responded by playfully pretending to push her husband away from her before throwing her arms around his neck.

"Now that's one for my notebook," Sam mumbled.

"Don't bet on it. That won't work on me, mister," Alex responded firmly, before adding, "I suggest we get back to our hotel before they find us."

"Alex, if they followed us here, trust me, they know where we're staying."

"So you're saying we don't go back to the hotel? Then we'd need to find Philippe and insist he takes us to this Mr. Anonymous or whatever his name is. We're being hunted and at the same time led down a rabbit hole to who knows where."

"Are you joining us for a late dinner and a nightcap? I know this great little brasserie in *Butte Montmartre* near the *Sacré Coeur.* The only place in Paris you truly experience romance."

"That sounds lovely, Etiénne, and hard to refuse, but we're going to bid you adieu and hope to see you again soon. Our evening was nothing but one to remember forever, thank you," Sam replied, and as the couples parted ways, Alex and Sam hastily set off in search of Philippe.

CHAPTER TEN

Confident their illustrious escape yielded them safe from their stalkers they followed the narrow graveled path as Etiénne had directed. The trail stretched its way between tall orange and cedar trees each marking the edge of their respective groves. Rich notes of nature's citrus perfume hung heavily in the air, and it wasn't long before they reached their marker. The Ceres Fountain wasn't as impressive as Josephine had made it out to be and consisted of a few bronzed statues in the center of a medium-sized square structure.

"Anything about this say 'summer' to you? Looks like a fancy frog pond to me," Sam commented.

Alex had thought the same but before she could respond the metal clanging sound of a bullet hitting the bronzed statue echoed through the thin night air. Forced to take the only cover available, Alex and Sam dropped face down behind the low wall surrounding the fountain. The unforeseen attack had caught them off their guard, affording them no time to draw their guns. Alex wrestled with the heavy baroque dress in an effort to reach for the firearm that she had strapped to her thigh underneath the skirt of her dress. Unable to do so, she flipped onto her back, narrowly escaping another bullet that hit the barely-there wall above her head. A brief second later and she yanked her gun from the holster and fired a single shot off over her head toward the direction the attack came from.

"Weasels! How did they find us?" Sam fumed as he pulled his gun from the small of his back.

"No idea, I thought we'd lost them. We're sitting ducks here, Sam. I'll go first, back toward the groves. Cover me!"

Sam fired off three bullets as Alex ran for the trees. Safely behind the thick trunk of a tall orange tree, she reciprocated until Sam reached the tree next to her. From their improved vantage point, they spotted the orange flashes of the gunmen hidden in the groves on the opposite side of the fountain. Another bullet flashed through the air and sliced through the skirt of Alex's huge dress. If she were to make it out alive, she'd have to dispose of the ridiculous costume which was affecting her mobility. Unable to undo the tiny buttons on the back of the dress, she instead used the rough bark of the tree and tore a small slit in the fabric just below her waist. As Sam fired off another two bullets, she ripped the fabric leaving her with a simple black slip dress she had had the sense to wear underneath.

"Much better!" Sam remarked mischievously, firing off another few shots, "but are you leaving it to me to do all the shooting here tonight? I'm almost out of bullets," he added.

But Alex's attention remained fixed on the tiny silver tracker barely visible in one of the buttons of her dress that now lay on the ground next to her.

"Get your clothes off!" she yelled at Sam as she took over from him and fired two bullets at one of the gunmen, hitting him in the shoulder.

"Did the French air get to you?"

"Strip, Sam! They've got trackers in."

With far less effort, it didn't take Sam long before he too was down to his boxers and a T-shirt.

"Let's make a run for it through the groves. I'm almost out of bullets. We'll head down the back on this side. Toss your clothes behind the next tree," Alex suggested.

The decoy worked, and while the pair ran toward the center of the grove behind them, the gunmen opened fire at the pile of clothes they'd thrown behind the trees opposite them. The lush foliage prevented any moonlight from penetrating the thick canopy above their heads as Alex and Sam ran in the direction of the palace between the dense trees. The night was eerily quiet, and the autumn chill summoned an opaque mist from the nearby stream that meandered between the giant trees behind them. The spiky heels of her shoes disappeared beneath the wet mulch that surrounded the trees—making it all the harder to run. She briefly stopped and broke the heels off her shoes. When they neared the place Etiénne had indicated the secluded VIP parking area was to the side of the palace, several drivers stood huddled under a large cedar tree nearby, their position only made visible by half a dozen glowing orange lights and the robust tobacco odored cloud that wafted in the chilly night breeze around them. As hoped for, the parked white Phantom was amongst a small fleet of VIP vehicles in the allocated parking area just inside the central gardens.

"There!" Sam pointed out; quickly spotting it amongst the pool of black and silver vehicles that flanked its sides.

"Do you think Philippe smokes?"

"All French men smoke as far as I know," Sam replied, "but we don't have much time to go find him amongst that bunch. Those thugs can't be far behind. With any luck, he's in the car waiting for us. Besides, may I remind you we're in our underwear."

Apart from the subdued chatter of the drivers who assembled at the furthest end of the parking area, there was no one else in sight. Approaching the car, they could just about make out Philippe's silhouette behind the steering wheel.

"Not in the mood to hang with the others, Philippe?" Sam

teased as he and Alex fell into the back seat. "Let's crack on, mate. We picked up some bad company inside," Sam said. Philippe didn't respond.

"Hey, Philippe, wake up, mate," Sam tapped on the window partitioning.

"Something's amiss, Sam."

Sam had sensed it too and was halfway out the car already, moments later yanking open the driver's door. "That's because the chap is dead."

"They got to him. Who are these people?"

"Not sure, but we need to get out of here before they catch us on camera with a dead body in hand and we end up in a Parisian prison in our underwear. Take Philippe's feet, Alex. Help me move him to the back seat. Hurry."

It didn't take them long to load the dead driver in the back of the car before Sam eagerly slipped behind the wheel joined by Alex in the passenger seat.

"This is a dream come true. I've always wanted to drive a Phantom."

"An innocent man is dead, Sam, not to mention he was our only link to Mr. Anonymous. How are we supposed to find the man now?"

"Do we have to? I mean, if we find him, I have to give back his car."

"Very funny. Are you going to drive this thing or let them catch up with us again?"

Alex flipped open the console between their seats and rummaged through a couple of old receipts. When her search turned up empty, she moved over to the glove box and paused when the automated cigar box popped open.

"Don't mind if I do, thank you," Sam motioned for her to hand him one of the expensive cigars while he turned the key in the ignition.

"Since when do you smoke?"

"I don't, but I've never driven a Rolls either, so I might as well live in the moment."

Alex ignored his witticism. She had come to know that her fiancée used his sharp wit and humor to conceal his discomfort and stress. It was how he managed to remain calm in extreme circumstances.

Still poking around in the glove box her hand settled on the cold metal she had become all too familiar with and seconds later she held a small silver and black revolver.

"Well, how about that. Why would a driver be carrying if he wasn't expecting danger?" Sam ventured suspiciously.

"Drive, Sam. We need to get out of here. We'll take a chance and go to our hotel. With the trackers gone, it buys us some time, but I'm not sure it will be for long. At least now we know how they've managed to be one step ahead all this time. If we're lucky, they're thinking we're still somewhere hiding in the gardens."

"Or not. Buckle up!"

Sam had spotted the four men approaching the parking lot from the corner of his eye and with no time to waste, backed out of the bay and sped off toward the long road leading out from the palace gates, leaving a giant cloud of dust in their wake.

"Whoever these guys are, they're good," Sam remarked as he watched them run for their car in the rear-view mirror. "Any idea where we should go?"

"No, there's nothing here. No vehicle registration papers, license, ID, not even a map … nothing."

"Well, we'd better find something, they are right behind us."

Alex swung around in her seat and spotted the silver Mercedes gaining on them. The road that led from Versailles was a long narrow road shouldered by rows of tall trees on either side.

"Can this fancy car go any faster?"

Sam didn't have to be invited twice. His foot pushed down on the accelerator, and the powerful engine roared down the road. And not a moment too soon. When the first bullets whistled through the air and hit the rear of their car, Alex slipped the magazine of her gun out into her hand.

"I'm almost out. Five at the most."

Another bullet hit the tailgate leaving a loud clanking noise to echo through the quietness of the night. She ducked down into the seat and Sam pushed down harder on the accelerator firing up all twelve of the Phantom's cylinders. As they neared the end of the road, he flicked a switch overriding the automatic gearbox to manual mode improving its maneuverability in doing so. Up ahead, a road sign signaled for them to turn left, heading toward Paris. The Phantom's tires screeched as they turned the corner. The road opened up into a two-lane highway that snaked its way through a residential suburb. Much to their regret, it wasn't long before they heard the screeching wheels of their huntsmen.

"We've got to shake these guys, Sam!" Alex switched her attention to the console in search of a button. "Where do you open this window?" She was referring to the glass partitioning between the front and rear seats. With Sam entirely focused on his driving as he turned another corner and Alex unable to locate the button on the console to open the panel, she thrust her gun's handle into the glass pane. It didn't shatter on the first blow, so she hit it again, this time with more force but still it didn't break.

"It's a shatterproof pane, Alex," Sam commented while he pushed a controller switch on the steering wheel. "Next time say please."

Alex snickered. "Hold it steady *please*, I'm climbing over."

It was a brief moment before Alex found herself in the backseat searching through Philippe's pockets. Another shot hit the rear window, leaving the slightest of dents in the glass.

"Well, what do you know? It's bulletproof," Sam announced with delight. "Hold on!" he warned as he dropped a gear, slammed on the brakes and swung the car around to face the shooters. The unexpected tactic forced their assailants to swerve to avoid hitting the Phantom head-on and in doing so, resulted in them losing control of their car. Alex and Sam watched as the silver Mercedes rolled several times before landing upside down off the shoulder of the road. Seconds later a thunderous noise reverberated through the streets when the car exploded into flames.

"Ha-ha! That'll teach them not to mess with us! Take that, you twits! Did you see that, love? Didn't know your fiancée had it in him, huh?"

"Great job, now please get us out of here before the police arrive," said Alex, taking up her place in the passenger seat again.

"Find anything while you were back there?"

Alex held out her fisted hand and slowly released her fingers, palm up.

CHAPTER ELEVEN

"He's one of them? Damn him! I actually liked the guy," Sam banged his hand on the steering wheel as they sped off.

"Don't beat yourself up, Sam. We should know by now, in this line of work, we can't trust anyone, ever!"

"I don't understand. Why bring us here, put us up in a fancy hotel, essentially treat us like royalty only to have us killed by his own men? It doesn't make sense. I don't buy it."

"I agree. Something doesn't add up. We need to find out what these chess pieces are and who this guy really is."

"Yeah, but how? Where do we even start? We have one dead man on the back seat, and we possibly left more back there, not to mention that we're driving in a stolen car."

Alex rolled the small brass pawn between her fingers and

stared out the window. "Stop! Pull over." She had spotted a clothing line on the small terrace of a ground floor apartment. It was well into the night, and all the lights were off. It seemed like an easy opportunity, and when Sam brought the car to a halt in the narrow street to the side of the apartment, Alex quietly slipped out and disappeared into the darkness. A mere minute later, she fell into the front seat with a matching pair of stone-washed jeans and a couple of shirts.

When they were back on the road again, Sam spoke, still tugging at the too-small jeans pinching his groin. "We're not far from the city. We're going to need to get rid of Philippe's body."

"Maybe the river? I saw some road signs back there."

Sam turned back and followed the road leading to the Seine, "Good idea, the last thing we need is the cops also hunting us down. We're going to need to weigh his body down, so he doesn't float. Not that I have experience in dumping dead bodies, but it's what they do on TV. I guess it makes sense, medically speaking."

When they reached the area by the river, they quickly discovered that it would be nearly impossible to dump the body without being spotted. Several houseboats were moored along the banks, and the corpse would most likely be caught on the guide ropes somewhere between them. They followed an arterial road to where it passed underneath a bridge, and a small secluded parking area sat snug between ample shrubbery directly on the banks of the river. Deciding it would be the most feasible of spots, they parked the car and pulled Philippe from the back seat, dragging his body behind the nearby concrete pillar that supported the bridge.

"Wait! I need his pants and shoes. These jeans will destroy any chance of having children with you," Sam said in a voice filled with guilt. "Besides it will just make him even more buoyant. Take off his jacket and shirt too and see if you can find some large stones or bricks lying around."

As they watched Philippe's corpse sink beneath the dirty green water of the Seine, police sirens shrieked in the distance.

"Let's get out of here," Alex urged.

For the next thirty minutes, they aimlessly drove through the streets of Paris. It was past three a.m. and, apart from the odd few young adults still enjoying a night out, the city was, for the most part, quiet. Neither Sam nor Alex spoke, each allowing the other to digest the night's events. It was only when the low vibrations of a mobile phone rang that the couple's thoughts were interrupted.

"Where's that coming from?" Alex whispered, "It's a phone. Listen."

Sam pulled the car off the road and homed in on the vibrations. "It's under my seat," he said, reaching down between his legs. The vibrations stopped as soon as Sam found the phone under his seat.

"He must have dropped it during the attack," Alex remarked. "Can you see who rang him?"

"No caller ID, and it gets worse. We need his thumb to get past the biometrics."

Alex sank back into her seat. "Does this car have Bluetooth? Maybe its synced."

"It does, but if it were, it would have rung through the car's speakers. Let's wait and see if he calls back. It might be Mr. A since Philippe never made it home."

"I've been thinking, Sam. We know someone in Paris who could help us. It's the only way. We're going to need to trust someone. I thought we'd make contact with DuPont."

"The guy from UNESCO who worked with ICCRU? I remember him. He seemed trustworthy, but then again, so did Philippe. It seems my judgment is lacking these days. How do you figure he'd be able to help us?"

"Well, I thought since he's involved in security, he might be able to trace the car's plates to an address."

Sam grinned broadly. "Anyone ever told you that you have the mind of a genius? That's the best idea I've heard all night. Let's give it a shot. What do we have left to lose?"

"We can use the emergency call button on the phone, right? They should be able to connect us."

"Think we could grab a bite to eat en route while you make contact? I'm ravenous."

♟

DuPont didn't hesitate to take their call, and within minutes Alex had an address and directions to a house situated in the 8th arrondissement in the city. According to DuPont, the car was registered to Maurice d'Andigné, one of the wealthiest aristocrats in France. As with the rest of the affluent suburb, the street in front of the three-story apartment block was deserted. A streetlamp flickered above their heads as they got out of the car.

"Looks like he's up," Alex said, pointing to the light in one of the rooms on the top floor.

"I'd be up all night too if I had this view in my front yard." Sam had his back to the apartment door and was staring at the Arc de Triomphe that towered out from behind a few tall trees directly in front of the building. "I bet he'll have a view of the Eiffel Tower too."

Alex rang the doorbell and waited. Her eyes trailed upward to the surveillance camera in the corner above the door and she rang again when no one answered. Still, there was no voice over the intercom box.

"Maybe we should just go in. I mean we are here to return the man's car, and it's not like he doesn't know who we are. He brought us here, remember?" Alex suggested.

"The door might be locked, but I guess you're right. It's worth a try."

But when Sam's hand leaned ever so gently against the door, it gave way.

"It's been open all along," Alex mouthed as she reached suspiciously for her gun and used the barrel to open the door wider. Their senses were at full alert as they entered the building greeted only by an empty, dark foyer. They walked back to back through the large room—each with their guns in position. Alex signaled for them to split up between the two gracious reception rooms on either side of the foyer. When the lower level delivered nothing but darkness, they met up at the marble staircase that led to the next floor. The impressive staircase had several steps that ended at a small landing and then divided into two sets of stairs—one to the east wing and one to the west. Using every skill learned from their tactical training, they proceeded with caution in opposite directions, checking each of the dark rooms along the long corridors. Again their sweep presented zero threats, leaving only the final floor above them unchecked. Alex tightened her grip on her gun. She recalled her magazine was almost empty and Sam silently communicated he estimated his to be even less than hers. There was no turning back now, and they slowly climbed the small flight of steps to the third floor. Once at the top, it was by this point in their partnership a well-practiced routine for Alex to step out first while Sam covered her, and after a small pause, they proceeded with skilled precision. The short corridor was empty. It was entirely dark like the rest of the apartment, apart from the low light they had spotted from the street coming from what seemed the only room on the floor. When they reached the room's doorway, Alex took a deep breath before quickly popping her head around into the room. It was his office and presented no immediate danger. Staying in position outside in the hallway, Alex mouthed to Sam, "Ready?" to which he nodded.

"Monsieur d'Andigné, it's Alex. May we come in? The door was open."

Hearing no reply, they remained in position, and Alex called out to the man again. The answer was the same. Sam signaled for them to go in, having assessed that there seemed little to no risk of a perpetrator being inside. To his mind, the man who appeared to be asleep in a red leather chair at his large wooden antique desk in the center of the room was alone. His assumption was correct. The somewhat small room in comparison to the rest of the house posed zero threat. Apart from the desk and red leather chair, there were only two floor-to-ceiling built-in bookcases on either side of the room and a wall that was given over entirely to large windows that overlooked the larger than life Arc de Triomphe in front of them.

Alex called out to Maurice d'Andigné again as she approached him from behind where he still sat unmoving in his chair. Her stomach turned when she reached him.

"Sam, we have a problem."

An ear to ear slit in the folds of his neck revealed the man had been murdered. Sam stared into the wound in d'Andigné's neck and with recalled medical expertise, volunteered his observations.

"It's fresh, so fresh I'd guess it happened within minutes of our arrival. He's still pumping out blood. Whoever did this knew what he was doing, that's for sure."

"How do you know?"

"He made sure he cut the external and internal jugulars. My guess is our host here never even saw it coming. It looks like a really thin exceptionally sharp knife was used, no ragged edges, no midway pause, clean from left to right. The guy bled out in minutes."

"Sam, what is going on here? I knew getting on that train was a bad idea. Dead bodies are turning up everywhere, and we're smack bang in the middle of it."

"Sweetheart, I have no idea, but I suggest we stay calm and see if we can find anything without leaving any fingerprints behind. There has to be something in this room that will help us understand who he is and why he sent you those messages in the first place."

"The way I see it, we are no longer on a fact-finding mission, Sam. We're fugitives. It's only a matter of time before they link us to both Philippe and now this guy."

Sam's eyes swept through the room. D'Andigné's desk was empty bar a couple of pens and a blank notepad. He crouched down to find a computer cable on the floor; one end still in the power socket.

"They took his laptop. Clearly, they were after something," Sam said to Alex, who was searching through the bookcases.

"Nothing here that I can see. Most of his books look like first editions. Quite the collection I'll tell you that much."

"This is interesting."

"What, Sam?"

"His signet ring. It's a black bishop, as in a chess piece."

Alex paced back over the red and gold Persian rug toward the desk and paused as her feet triggered a creak in the floorboards. She stepped back over it. It was the same noise that had been annoying her since the safe under her floor was installed.

"I've got something," she said, announcing her find to Sam as she started rolling up the rug from one end until she rested on the spot roughly halfway down the middle of the rug.

"Of course, he had yours installed after all."

Familiar with the trigger mechanism to open the floor-boards, Alex knelt and clicked the underfloor safety box open. As their eyes took sight of the light-brown leather suitcase safely hidden under the floor, they heard the police sirens approaching.

"Grab it! We need to get out of here," Sam urged, before hurriedly concealing the safe under the carpet again.

Just as they reached the bottom of the stairs, the flashing blue and red police lights announced they were too late to escape through the front door.

"This way," Alex yelled, heading through to the kitchen where she led him down into the private parking garage she'd discovered when they first entered the apartment.

"Take your pick," Alex motioned to Sam when they were met with three more shiny vehicles while she pushed the manual button on the wall to open the garage.

"Don't mind if I do," Sam said with glee as he slipped behind the wheel of a slinky steel-grey sports car.

"Come on, Sam. They're about to come down those stairs any second."

"There are no keys! It's biometric."

"We don't have time to check the others, Sam, let's go. We'll have to do this one on foot."

Alex was still in position with her hand on the button. "Come on, come on!"

The quick closing garage door afforded them just enough time to slip underneath undetected, and the pair escaped on foot into the dark streets behind the building.

CHAPTER TWELVE

S oft droplets of rain settled on her brows as Alex ran beside Sam along the quiet streets. Her newly transformed silk pumps that complemented the ball gown she had worn earlier were drenched, and the wet male shirt she got from the washing line, only exacerbated the chilly night air. She tightened her grip around the handle of the small leather suitcase. The rain made it slippery. Soft streetlights illuminated the vapors expelled from their lungs as they kept running.

When the rain came down harder, and it became increasingly more difficult not to slip on the smooth cobbled roads, they ducked under the shelter of a nearby bus stop. At that moment, Alex had never felt more lost or helpless, and she sensed Sam, who was usually quick to come up with solutions, was feeling the same. They were cold, wet, and tired as they huddled together on the narrow bench.

"What are we going to do, Sam? The sun will be up soon."

"Shh, let's not worry about that right now. Let's rest and dry up for a few minutes. I doubt anyone will come looking for us here. Hopefully, the rain will stop soon."

S am jolted when he felt someone kick the sole of his shoe and woke to see an elderly French woman go off at them. From her body language, he could tell she was displeased with them turning the bus stop into a homeless shelter. The woman's shrill voice woke Alex too, whose elementary French managed to calm the woman down enough to stop kicking at Sam's feet and leave. Thankfully the rain had stopped. Around them, the city's morning activities were in full swing. Pedestrians rushed along the sidewalks to work, and the smell of fresh-baked bread and coffee tantalized their empty stomachs.

"What time is it?" Alex asked, suddenly alert and on edge.

"Got to be somewhere in a hurry? Relax. It's not like we have anywhere to go, sweetheart."

"We can't stay here or keep roaming the streets of Paris. We're going to have to risk it and get back to the hotel to get our passports."

"No need, I've got them right here, my dear." Sam lifted his shirt to reveal the small pouch he had strapped to his torso.

"You've had them there all along?"

"Yep," he said, grinning with satisfaction. "I've learned a thing or two along the way. Always be prepared, right? Got our cash too."

Alex kissed him on the cheek. "What do you say we try to get something to eat then? Now might be the perfect time for that omelet you never had back home."

A nearby street café buzzed with friendly Parisian flair and Alex and Sam took an intimate table in the corner of the shop. As was typically preferred all over Europe, apart from a few occupied tables that stood alongside the window, most of the customers sat at the tiny tables on the curb outside. Alex couldn't delay the inevitable anymore and unclipped the latch to the suitcase. She lifted the glass object that lay snugly between red velvet cushioning from the suitcase. It measured roughly ten inches in height and about five in width weighing no more than about three pounds. The base was made from a wood she guessed to be walnut upon which a glass dome was attached. Inside, a smaller object was held in position by a black metal rod. Dark brown with a burgundy tinge she immediately recognized it.

"It's the heart, isn't it? The one he sent me in the picture on the phone." Sam nodded.

"Is it real?"

"Not sure, I'd have to open it up to be certain. It could just be a replica, but without touching and inspecting it up close, there's no way of knowing for sure. People are quite crafty these days."

Alex inspected the wooden base and tried twisting it as if she was opening a jar of apricot preserve.

"Here, let me try."

But the result was the same when Sam tried. "Seems the only way in is to break the glass."

"No! That will jeopardize its value."

"Really, Alex? You're worried about preserving its value over trying to get us out of the situation we've found ourselves in?"

"Not necessarily but there's got to be another way, Sam. It's not like they had superglue back then."

Alex took back the encased organ and stared into the wooden base. The rounded sides were smooth and free from any vignettes or markings of any kind. Underneath, a thin layer of dark green felt fabric covered the underside of the base. It was ever so slightly raised in places, and Alex gently ran her fingers across the wooly cloth. Excitement rushed through her body as her fingertips traced the edges of a small square. She grabbed the knife from the table and carefully picked at the corner of the fabric until it peeled away from the wood to reveal a piece of paper folded into a small square.

"It looks like a letter." Alex squealed with excitement and placed the heart back into the suitcase before gently unfolding the paper. The yellowed paper was perfectly intact, and she spread it out onto the table. Penned in grey ink which, judging from the ink blotches across the page, indicated that it was done with a quill or perhaps even an early creation of the fountain pen, and dated August 1805 it was simply signed off as *R.J. Pinoir II.*

"I can't understand a single bit of this! My French isn't that good, but if I'm not mistaken, then it's the same traditional French from the newspaper clipping d'Andigné sent to me."

"Any chance we could get it to your contact back home? The one who helped you out with the first one."

"Not likely, no. Without me being able to meet face to face with the man, it would have to pass through too many hands to get to him. We can't risk anything now."

"Well, then I guess that only leaves DuPont. We'll have to pay the guy a visit and hope for the best. He might understand it."

"You're right, come on then."

It was a short bus ride to DuPont's office near the Louvre museum, and Alex and Sam were told to wait for him in the small reception area outside his office. His secretary, a young raven-haired girl with legs up to her neck, impeccably dressed in a tight black skirt that ended just above her knees and a translucent yellow chiffon blouse, glanced suspiciously at the poorly dressed pair on the couch. Alex was sure the sizeable well-arranged bouquet with soft pink roses and lavender on the coffee table in front of them did nothing to mask the odor their bodies emitted into the small space either. Feeling unduly aware of herself, Alex combed her fingers through her tangled hair and tucked one side behind her ear. She wasn't the jealous type, but she couldn't help wondering if Sam's eyes appreciated the girl's appearance. She glanced at him where his nose was deep between the pages of a medical magazine he'd found on the table next to the couch and smiled inwardly as she realized he had no interest in the girl at all.

The phone on the desk bleeped, and Alex watched as the girl lifted the receiver to her ear. An instant later, she rose and beckoned for them to follow her into DuPont's office— he had already left his desk to meet them at the door. As was the tradition in Europe, DuPont kissed the air above each of Alex's ears and, in true energetic form, ushered them to take a seat before slipping into his chair behind his desk.

"You remember Sam Quinn?"

"Oui-oui, of course. And now I can give you a proper congratulations on your engagement."

"I'm sorry to disturb you again, Jean-Pierre, but we have nowhere else to turn. We need your help."

"But of course," DuPont answered through pouted lips accompanied by his usual Gallic shrug.

"We found a letter that we need help translating. It's in French and dates back to 1805."

Alex placed the small case on her lap and flipped it open. She heard DuPont draw in a sharp breath when his eyes caught sight of the artifact, but he remained quiet, watching as she pulled the letter from the secret envelope under the green cloth.

She unfolded the letter and gently smoothed it out onto the glass desk in front of him. DuPont hooked a small pair of spectacles over his ears, rose, and leaned in as he examined the letter more carefully. He hovered like that for several minutes with his hands behind his back, as if he was too scared to touch it and then eventually spoke in a nervous voice.

"Where did you find this?"

"In Maurice d'Andigné's apartment—last night. He's dead."

DuPont removed his spectacles and took a step back.

"What does it say?" Sam asked, the tone of his voice lower than usual.

"It's a confession."

"To what?" It was Alex's turn.

DuPont seemed suddenly withdrawn and equally nervous.

"What does it say, DuPont? A confession to what?" Sam repeated sternly.

"I'm not sure, but leave it with me. I will contact you once I know for sure."

Alex picked up the letter, "You know I can't do that, Jean-Pierre. I think you know what it says. Why don't you want to tell us?"

"I can't, Alex, it's protocol."

"Protocol! You're joking. What protocol, DuPont? Tell us what it says." Sam spoke with urgency, his voice carrying more frustration than he had intended.

DuPont slammed one hand down onto his desk, sending a clanging sound similar to that of metal hitting glass into the air.

"I can't, okay?"

Alex felt her heart skip several beats as her eyes took hold of the piece of jewelry on his little finger.

"Thanks for your time, Jean-Pierre. We'll find another way," Alex said, maintaining her composure and hastily closing the case. Sam had noticed the ring too and followed Alex toward the door. Halfway there the pair froze when they heard the familiar sound a revolver makes when you pull back the hammer to cock it.

"I can't let you take it, Alex. Please hand it over. I don't want to have to shoot you."

Alex and Sam slowly turned to see DuPont standing behind his desk with a small revolver in his hand.

"What is it with all you people? Is there no one left on this planet who cares more about the world than themselves?" Alex exclaimed.

"You leave me no choice, Alex. Hand it over." DuPont moved toward them.

"Fine," Alex placed the suitcase on the floor in front of her and folded her arms across her chest.

DuPont took the bait and reached for the case. Alex jerked her knee up, colliding with his jaw making him stumble back onto the floor at which time Sam kicked the gun from his hand.

"You idiots! You don't know who you're messing with! They'll kill you! They'll kill me too!"

"Who DuPont? Who is trying to kill us?" Alex hissed, but DuPont remained silent.

"Grab his gun, Alex! We don't have time to play games with this guy. Last chance, DuPont. Speak up," he tried again, but still, DuPont refused to answer, and Sam jammed his right fist into DuPont's face rendering him unconscious on the floor.

"You okay?"

"Fine, let's just get out of here before I do something I'll regret," Alex answered.

With the office door quietly closed behind them, Alex informed the girl that her boss had asked not to be disturbed and that she was to hold all his calls. The naive girl didn't query it and promptly returned to her keyboard.

The duo made a run for the exit, choosing to descend the two floors via the stairwell instead of using the elevator. Apart from one guard in the foyer, the office building had few security measures in place. When they entered the lobby, they spotted the guard on his two-way radio and ducked into an empty meeting room.

"He knows," Alex whispered.

"The girl must have checked in on DuPont. No way the guy is already conscious."

Relieved to have the safety of the small meeting room, Alex checked the barrel in DuPont's revolver. "It's full."

"Good, something tells me we might need it," he said, peeping through the small window in the door. "We're going to have to take our chances and make a run for it before the police get here. I can't see the guard, but the exit is unattended. I'll carry the case. Ready?"

Alex nodded as she handed him the case and pushed the small revolver into the pocket of her jeans. Sam yanked open the door, and the couple sprinted across the foyer, narrowly escaping the guard who had come out of nowhere directly behind them. His panicked voice shouted for them to stop, but Alex and Sam had already slipped through the exit and disappeared into a group of pedestrians crossing the street.

Behind them, the police had pulled up to the building sending a multitude of excited screams from a small group of Chinese tourists on the sidewalk—now eagerly snapping away with their cameras. In the distance, they heard the police ordering them to stop, but they kept running. The iconic glass pyramid structure outside the Louvre stretched out in front of them. Relieved that the expansive plaza surrounding it was bustling with tourists and visitors they used it to their advantage and headed toward the more crowded corners. Female screams alerted them that the police were not far behind.

Caught between the police gaining from behind and the entrance to the museum in front of them, they had reached the end of the large public square. The pair searched for the best way out.

"This way!" Sam pointed Alex toward the large bridge that ran over the nearby Seine.

Faced with having to cross a bustling roundabout they raced between the oncoming cars which seemed to have no partic-ular direction and caused several small collisions in doing so. Sam ran in front and navigated them to the pedestrian walkway that ran alongside the bridge. Just then two police vehicles pushed into the roundabout directly behind them. Their feet thumped hard on the pink-tinged walkway. Narrowly missing a few oncoming cyclists, they forged forward. Behind them, gaining fast, the police made it through the congested traffic onto the bridge. Now in a frantic state, their eyes searched in a futile attempt to find an alternative escape route knowing they could never outrun the police. Much to their disappointment, they spotted more police cars approaching them from the opposite side of the bridge. Wedged between law enforcement officers fast approaching them from both sides, Sam and Alex stopped, frozen in time in the middle of the bridge. It was Alex who spotted the approaching houseboat on the river cruising underneath the bridge. With unspoken words, as if they shared one mind, they turned and jumped.

CHAPTER THIRTEEN

S am hit the flat wooden deck of the long narrow barge first, shortly followed by Alex. Behind them the skipper frantically cussed at them from behind his wheel. Alex leaped across the deck and pushed her gun into the angered captain's ribs instructing him to speed it up. The man did as he was told. From the bridge, the police ordered them to stop, but Alex thrust her gun harder into the captain's side and pushed the boat's throttle full speed ahead. The police fired off a shot hitting the stern directly behind them. It was clearly intended as a warning shot to frighten them into surrender. Instead, it resulted in the skipper attempting to wrestle Alex for the gun. Fully antici-pating his reaction, Alex responded by breaking his nose with a backward jab of her elbow. The man squealed with pain before Alex knocked him unconscious with a sturdy left hook to his jaw. Another warning shot from the police hit one of the engines, narrowly missing its propeller. But as the distance slowly grew between the boat and the bridge, Alex and Sam managed to elude the police once again.

The luxury eighty-foot private longboat powered at its limited top speed through the once calm waters of the Seine. In its wake, waves threatened to capsize a couple on their kayaks sending more than a few obscene hand gestures their way, and Alex slowed it down to the permissible four mph speed limit. Apart from the skipper, there was no one else on board. Sam had dragged the wretched man below deck where he gagged and tied him to the small built-in diner.

"You certainly showed him who is in charge. The poor chap is lights out," Sam stepped back on deck with two brandies in hand. "Thought you might want some sustenance." He handed her a glass before adding. "This is where Bond would disappear with the girl below deck, by the way."

Alex threw back the strong French liquor. "Bond didn't have an audience that could wake up at any time and let's not forget we're not exactly out of danger yet, Sam. What are we going to do with the guy when he wakes up?"

"We should dump him."

"In the water? He'll drown. I'm not a murderer."

"No, I meant, we should drop him off, onshore. He'll wake up and find his way home."

"And how long do you think before they track us down on the boat? I wouldn't be surprised if the police already put barricades up further down the river."

Sam didn't answer. Instead, he stuck his hand into a narrow compartment behind the wheel and pulled out a map. Alex watched while he flipped it over, unfolded one side and folded in another.

"There." He pointed to a particular spot on the map. "That's a canal, one of several that run through Paris. We'll drop the captain off somewhere here to throw them off our trail and then make our way back to this canal over here. They can't possibly have men on each canal. My guess is they'll focus on the main thoroughfares for now. It will, at the very least, buy us some time, and God knows we need that right now."

Alex smiled, briefly placing her head on his shoulder. She could always count on Sam's ability to think under pressure. He was right. They desperately needed time to rethink their plan. Too much had happened, and they were entirely in the dark.

When they managed to successfully leave the still unconscious skipper on an empty mooring in the shade of a large leafy tree, they turned the boat and headed back for the canal as planned. Since the river was bustling with tourist boats and private charters, they remained alert and on guard. As luck would have it, the private boat was fully stocked with food and a small collection of men's attire. They continued down the narrow canal without stopping, briefly taking turns behind the wheel to afford each other a short break for a quick shower and clothing change.

"Look what I found—the skipper's laptop." Alex settled into the chair next to Sam where he was at the wheel. "I thought I'd start a search on the guy who wrote the letter."

It wasn't long after typing in the author's name that Alex found what she was looking for. Reading her findings out loud, she continued searching via the online search engine.

"It says here that *R.J. Pinoir II* was the son of the doctor who performed the autopsy on the uncrowned King of France. Louis Charles died from tuberculosis in the Temple prison at the age of ten on June 8, 1795."

"DuPont said it was a confession. What could the son of the medical examiner possibly be confessing to? Makes no sense."

"Wait, there's more. Apparently, the doctor, *R.J. Pinoir* I, kept the boy's heart. Says he wrapped it in his handkerchief and later stored it in alcohol as a souvenir. It was then stolen by one of his students who, on his deathbed, had an attack on his conscience and had his wife return it to the Archbishop of Paris where it stayed until the palace was later attacked in the Revolution of 1830."

"So if anyone had anything to confess it would have been the student who stole it from the doctor," Sam commented.

"Then that means this letter is simply the son reporting that his father had stolen the heart in the first place or knowledge of the student who stole it from him in turn. Of which neither is very significant this late in the game. So why was it under lock and key, and how did d'Andigné get hold of the heart?"

"See what you can dig up on him. A guy with that much money has to be associated with something."

Alex typed his name into the search field. "Um, just that he's extremely wealthy with a net worth of fifty-three billion Euros—that's roughly fifty-nine billion dollars. He's a chairman and major shareholder of a retail conglomerate but made his money as an art collector and owns one of the largest collections of post-Impressionist art worldwide. Never got married."

"An art collector. That explains how he might have come to have the heart. Maybe he bought it at an auction somewhere along the line."

"And hid it under his floorboards. What for? It's not the Mona Lisa, Sam."

"Perhaps, but he might have also discovered the letter. DuPont did seem rather nervous, not to mention that he pointed a gun at us and was prepared to kill us for it."

"You're right. But there's nothing clandestine about a confession that's been out there for centuries is there? I mean, so what? He did the autopsy, stole the boy's heart, and kept it as a souvenir—big deal. The boy was already dead and buried. That's not much of a secret to confess to or keep hidden. I don't think any of this has to do with the letter. DuPont didn't just want the letter. He wanted the heart also."

"True, and it is, in fact, a picture of the heart d'Andigné sent you not the letter. I think we're onto something. Anything there on the chess pieces? I find it bizarre that both Maurice d'Andigné and DuPont wore identical rings. D'Andigné's ring had a bishop, and DuPont had a knight in his. Whereas, the guys on the train and Philippe had pawns. It has to mean something."

Alex clicked away on the laptop in search of some answers, but it turned up empty. "Nothing, just a whole lot on how to play chess. I can't even find a similar ring on eBay."

She slammed the laptop shut. "Now that d'Andigné's dead we'll never know why he lured us here. None of this is making any sense."

"Let's think this through, Alex. The man sent you a letter saying he needs your help. Then a newspaper article informing you of the dauphin's existence and that he died, taking the monarchy with him. After that, you get the picture of the heart."

"Exactly, and then everything turned into shambles, and we're right in the middle of it with dead bodies everywhere. Including his, if I might add."

"I think we can safely rule out that it was d'Andigné who had us followed or tried to kill us. Whoever is after us killed him, and I suspect they are the same ones who were after the suitcase. It's the heart that's important; at least enough to kill for and scare DuPont into pointing a gun at our heads. I'd also guess that whoever has him scared must be extremely powerful. DuPont is pretty well protected by several military agencies and governments."

Alex ran her palms up and down over her face as if she was washing it with invisible soap before she spoke again.

"What if Etiénne's theories aren't just his family's passed down tales? What if there's truth in it?" Alex ventured.

"You mean the part where the boy escaped and lived? That he never died?"

"Exactly. He did say no one ever saw the boy's body. What if it's all a cover-up?"

"You're talking about something that happened more than two centuries ago, Alex. That would be quite a cover-up that can be successfully kept under wraps for more than two hundred years. And by whom? Why? I'd say that's pretty impossible to pull off. I don't buy it. We're missing something."

"I guess you're right. After all, we have the boy's heart right here. Can't get more proof than that."

Alex got up and rested her arms over the railing as she stared out into the streets along the canal. Her eye caught the movement of a police vehicle—they'd just been spotted.

"We've been made, Sam. You've got to get us out of these narrow walkways."

Alex pulled out the map and traced her finger along the blue lines marking the canals.

"We're trapped, Sam. We've been going around in a massive circle surrounding the city. The smaller waterways will slow us down too much."

The sudden splash of a bullet hitting the water to the right of her had both of them duck down behind the wheel.

"Behind us, Sam!" Alex warned as she spotted a speedboat, moments before another bullet clanked against the deck, mere feet away from where they were standing. Alex fired back a shot which pierced their attacker's cabin window. In the street, alongside them, the police vehicle accelerated toward the approaching bridge.

"There!" Alex pointed to a small waterway not marked on the map for which the reasons became apparent soon after they took it. It was a dead ending onto a private mooring, which in turn, led directly into an apartment. Alex snatched a waterproof pouch from one of the small compartments and secured the heart inside. Sam watched as she hastily flipped all the nearest buoys into position over the railing before proceeding to run along the deck and doing the same with the rest of them.

"Get ready to jump, Sam," she yelled when she met up with him and forced the boat at full throttle into reverse gear.

"Now!"

They jumped and swam away from the boat toward the mooring and where they hid under the small wooden jetty. The longboat pushed back, colliding every so often with the narrow walls before regaining its course along the canal. Guided by the orange inflatables bouncing the boat away from the walls, it picked up speed. From the tiny gap underneath the jetty, Alex and Sam heard the attacker's boat approaching the canal's entrance and moments later the loud thumping sound of the two boats colliding sent rippling waves through the water toward them. The barge's powerful engines roared as it forced its way into the attacker's boat and mere seconds later, a thunderous explosion echoed through the short canal. When the second explosion hit, the ingenious couple cautiously swam their way through the channel toward the accident scene. As they neared the carnage, two dead bodies floated upside down in the water close by. From the low bridge, the police leaned over the sides in search of Alex and Sam while reporting the incident on their radios. On the opposite side, onlookers curiously lined up along the street.

"Think these might come in handy now," Sam gloated as he handed Alex one of two small emergency scuba tanks.

"Anyone ever told you how smart you are, Sam Quinn?"

"Not recently, but how about we get out of here, and you can tell me again over a baguette later."

Hidden by the dark brown waters of the canal, they took to their underwater passage and managed to evade the law undetected.

CHAPTER FOURTEEN

They swam for a solid fifteen minutes. Exhausted, cold, and with their eyes stinging from the filthy canal waters, they crawled out onto a narrow footpath underneath a small overhanging pedestrian bridge. Flanked by the canal on the one side and a steep embankment covered in grass, they took to hiding behind the concrete bridge support.

"So much for getting all cleaned up." Sam broke the tension as a bicycle's wheels whirred across the bridge over their heads.

Alex unzipped the airtight pouch to find the relic still perfectly intact. It was late afternoon, and the air was chilly. The suburb seemed tranquil, apart from a few bicycles crossing the bridge. Unable to control her chattering teeth as her body fought against the cold, Alex wrung the excess water from her hair and duplicated the process with her pants and shirt.

"We need to get you out of these wet clothes and dried up before hypothermia sets in. Your skin is practically purple." Sam's hands searched for the pouch with their passports and cash, relieved to feel it just below his pants' waistband where he'd taped it inside a zip-sealed freezer bag.

"Any idea where we are?" Alex spoke as another shiver engulfed her frozen body.

"Not a clue but it looks to be a smaller village. Perhaps exactly what we need to stay out of sight for now."

They followed the footpath along the embankment to where it eventually ran into five stone steps leading up into the street. Further down the quiet street, a fresh food market buzzed with traders selling their local produce and crafts. It presented the perfect opportunity for them to get dry clothes and food. The swift walk brought about a positive impact on Alex's body temperature transforming her purple skin almost entirely with a pink blush to her cheeks. Sam increased their pace as he navigated their way to a table displaying several used clothing items; sold to them in aid of the local hospice. It wasn't long before the pair disappeared into an alleyway and changed into their new attire. Grateful for the warmth that slowly percolated through their bodies, they set off back to the market in search of finding a replacement suitcase and something to eat. In and amongst the array of traders' tables, as they paused next to a spread of cheese and cold meats, Alex caught sight of a stall which displayed a large assortment of books and magazines. Her eyes settled on the cover of a magazine displaying a charred French flag that lay on the ground between a group of men wearing black suits with matching masks. Intrigued, she picked it up and read the heading.

La Fraternité - Vérité ou Mensonge

Her fingers flipped to the index page until she found the title which translated to 'The Fraternity — Truth or Lies' and then continued through the pages about midway into the magazine. Engrossed with finding the article, she hadn't heard the stall owner's grumpy appeal for her to buy the magazine instead of reading it for free. He snatched it from her hand and smacked it back down onto the table with the rest. Alex leaned across the table to pick it up again increasing the angry Frenchman's agitation. Sam leaned over and shoved a note down onto the table, snatching up the magazine after doing so. "Let's get out of here, Alex, before this guy attracts unnecessary attention."

Working their way through the crowded market, they moved toward a small patch of green grass at the edge of the canal.

"What's so important about this magazine that you had to get it?" Sam asked as they settled down onto a nearby park bench.

"I'm not sure. Might be nothing, but I have a hunch," Alex said as she bit into a large chunk of cheese and broke off a piece of bread. She flipped open the magazine and set about reading the first paragraph.

"And?"

"I'm still trying to figure it out but, judging by the few words I do understand, it's about a secret fraternity who call themselves *The Resistance*. According to this article, it seems they've been around for centuries and that some say they're just a myth while others believe them to have existed since…"

Alex stopped.

"Since what?" Sam urged.

"Since the French Revolution," Alex answered with a subdued voice. "Sam, I think these are the people who have been after us. Since the French Revolution, Sam!"

"Now hold on, Alex. It could just be a coincidence. The Revolution marked a lot of change, so it doesn't mean anything. What else does it say?"

"There's a lot of words I don't understand, but I think it says something along the lines that, though many believe it to be nothing but a fable, there are those who have claimed to have been part of them but managed to break free. That they are in hiding in fear of being found and killed. Sam, we need to find someone who used to be part of this group."

"And how do you intend doing that, sweetheart. It's not as if their names are listed in a central directory."

Alex flipped back and forth between the two pages. Her eyes fell on the name of the journalist. She flipped to the front cover noticing the date was only a year old.

"We need to find this journalist. Reporters always have sources. He might not give us a name, but perhaps he could arrange a meeting between us. It's our only shot, Sam. If we don't find these people first, they'll find us. And I don't think I need to remind you that they'll kill us. It's very evident we have something they're after. We're going to need to get ahead of them if we're to survive."

Sam paused while he deliberated the consequences.

"Fine, but I'd feel a lot better if we can get our hands on more ammunition. Just to be sure."

When the couple had eaten their fill, they lay low until nightfall. The village was eerily quiet. It was as if the bustling market square from earlier never existed.

"Where is everyone? There's not a single pub or restaurant open," Sam commented.

"Looks like a ghost town, doesn't it? Not even the apartment lights are on."

"I think everyone gets to bed early and rises early. I was

hoping we'd stumble upon some gangs that could help with getting us some ammo."

"Maybe we're too early. Or in the wrong place."

They chose a side street that led toward the Metro, and it wasn't long before they took to the dark stairway leading to the underground train station. Graffiti covered walls ushered them through the poorly lit subway. Marked by loud male voices and their amber cigarette tips, as expected, a few thugs stood huddled against the wall just as Alex and Sam turned the corner. Most people stumbling upon a gang this late at night would be intimidated and turn back, but by now, Alex and Sam were well equipped to handle them—with or without guns. As the pair approached, the gang stopped laughing, slowly dispersing their tight circle. It was evident they were in the mood to cause trouble. Alex and Sam walked directly toward them, their upright demeanor sending the gang a message of their own; that they were there to do business. Two of the young men, appearing to be around nineteen or twenty at the most, took a step forward, shielding three more behind them. The taller of the two had his hands in his black bomber jacket's pockets, exposing his pants that hung low across his backside. He stuck out his chin, silently asking the question as to what Alex and Sam wanted. It was Alex who spoke in a low, confident tone.

"We're looking to buy some equipment."

The gang member ran his eyes to her feet and back up to her face.

"You a cop?" he questioned suspiciously.

"No, just need to restock our supplies."

"What makes you think we can help you."

"Can you?"

"Maybe. Depends."

"On what?"

"What are we talking? Semi-automatic, rifles…"

"Semi's would do, untraceable of course, and enough bullets."

"It's not cheap."

"We're good for it. When can you have it?"

The young man turned to get a nod from one of his associates.

"Follow us."

With negotiations completed, Alex and Sam followed the small group of young men back toward the entrance of the tunnel. Although their initial thoughts were to negotiate that they had them deliver the guns to them, Alex and Sam had quickly assessed the group presented no threat. It was highly unlikely they were in cahoots with their assailants. Across the subway, a small narrow street took them in between more graffitied walls, passing several abandoned shopfronts. Above their heads, washing hung from the balconies of what appeared to be council apartments while the faint thudding of beatbox music disturbed the peaceful quiet of the small village. With half the gang in front of them and the other half behind them, Alex and Sam cautiously continued, testing their abilities to trust these complete strangers to the max. When the streets grew even darker, and the buildings narrowed to reveal a short alley, Alex slipped her hand into her jacket pocket to where she had hidden DuPont's revolver. It had been exposed to the water from the canal so there was no way of knowing if it would still fire, but at the very least, it should be enough to scare an attacker off. A minute later, the dark alley ended in front of what appeared to be the backdoor of a shop that seemed wholly abandoned and neglected. The gang stopped, turning around to do one final assessment on whether their new clients' were indeed to be trusted. Content with their findings, they knocked out a coded sequence of rhythmic sounds on the hollow steel door and waited. The door swung open, almost instantly, and a fat, near sumo-like figure, greeted them. Unlike the youths, he wasn't French and resembled someone of Brazilian descent. The much older man, roughly around his mid-thirties, invited the party in without hesitation.

Inside, a narrow passage led them through to where it opened up into a medium-sized shop floor. A dense layer of tobacco smoke hung thick in the air, making it nearly impossible to see to the front of the shop apart from the ability to see that the windows and door were painted black.

At one end, five men sat around a square table playing poker. On the other side, two large red couches stood in an L-shape along the wall. A mirrored coffee table positioned in front of it was cluttered with a massive assortment of drugs and narcotics paraphernalia. Knelt next to it were three girls, likely to be prostitutes since their clothing left little to the imagination. The sound of a toilet flushing had Alex and Sam turn to where a door flung open behind them and a shorter than average man entered the room. His pitch-black hair was combed back into a short, sleek style. Dressed in an orange floral shirt, entirely unbuttoned, over a sleeveless black vest with black pants, he finished fastening his belt buckle. As with the others, he too appeared to be Brazilian. Much to their surprise, Alex and Sam watched as his hand reached around the saggy-pants youth's neck and pulled him into a warm embrace. As suspected, they both spoke Portuguese, and soon, the room turned into a joyful place of welcoming. When the pleasantries ceased, the short man turned his attention to where Alex and Sam patiently waited. With his hands on his hips, he walked across the room and paused in front of them. Now up close, Alex fought back the urge to laugh at the clichéd gold necklace and multitude of rings that adorned his body.

The boy spoke behind him, and Alex and Sam got the same lingering glance-over received by the youth earlier. A brief nod toward his sumo sidekick had the man walk across the room to where he was waiting in front of a large steel cupboard in the corner.

"Where's the money?" the short man asked in a high-pitched voice.

"First show me what you've got," Alex responded immediately.

The man called out a name, and one of the men at the table rose to his feet. His face was adorned with several piercings, and a substantial tattoo of a rose lay across his neck. He joined the big guy in front of the steel cupboard and flung open both steel doors. He proceeded to pull out three firearms and spoke in a low, raspy voice.

"We have a Sig P226 with double-action and a side-mounted decocker. This one is the Colt M1911, and this is your standard Glock 17. Each with one hundred bullets and spare clips."

This time Sam spoke, "We'll take it all," he said, producing a wad of cash from his pocket and handing it over. Alex shoved their purchases next to the encased heart in their backpack and Sam secured it on his back. Based on the saggy-pants youth's reaction, the cash was quite visibly more than they had anticipated getting. Winning favor from his ringleader and with an easy payday under the belt, they rapidly ushered Sam and Alex back out toward the alley.

Relieved the transaction had gone down smoothly, Sam pulled Alex under his arm. "What do you say we try to find ourselves a place to get some shut-eye?"

Alex agreed. Since leaving London neither of them had any sleep, apart from stealing an hour here and there.

"I could've done with testing out that king-sized bed back at the fancy hotel. Pity we never got to live it up in there fully," Sam said.

"Oh, something tells me you'll find a way to make up for it. For now, I'll settle for a park bench since all the lodges have closed for the night."

CHAPTER FIFTEEN

Relieved to be woken by the noise of early commuters instead of a kick in the shin by a grumpy elderly woman, Sam planted a gentle kiss on Alex's head.

"Wake up sleepyhead. Time to get cracking."

Surprised she'd slept so soundly, Alex sat up and took in the busyness of the morning. It was barely daybreak, but the dawn of the new day brought a new-found excitement to her soul.

"Think this town has an internet café?"

"I'm sure it will, although I doubt it will be open this early. I guess we could try."

But unlike the desolate impression the village had painted the night before, the streets were alive with commuters as soon as they turned the corner into the main square. Lively chatter spilled from the street cafés and, bar a few clothing boutiques, most of the shops were already open.

"What time is it?" Alex queried, as surprised as Sam.

"Barely seven thirty a.m. Bizarre isn't it?"

"Told you they know how to appreciate life here. We have it all wrong."

It wasn't long before a handwritten sign in a nearby much quieter café announced it had internet facilities. Discounting the fact that it was a far cry from the internet facilities they were used to, it would suffice, and while Sam ordered two croissants and a couple of coffees to go, Alex quickly slipped in behind the computer. The reporter's name turned out to be quite a common one, delivering more than fifty namesakes in her search. She pulled the magazine from the rucksack and cross-referenced the title to that of the tabloid. Absorbed with her activities, Sam suddenly whispered, turning his back toward the barista.

"Keep your head down. We need to go."

"I'm still looking."

"There's no time. We need to go," Sam said with more urgency as he anxiously watched the barista turn another page. He had started reading the paper from the back as most sport enthusiasts did. One more page flip and he'd be reaching the front page.

Alex only had to look up briefly to notice the black and

white photo of them next to one of Maurice d'Andigné's on the front page of the barista's newspaper.

"Almost done." She pushed on as Sam once again urged their departure.

"Got it!" she exclaimed, memorizing the address before wiping the search history.

But, by the time they reached the front of the shop, the barista had already recognized the fugitives and summoned the police.

"We're innocent!" Alex yelled back at him before running across the street.

No sooner had they reached the previous night's rendezvous point in the subway when loud police sirens rang through the crisp morning air. Their feet thumped loudly in the confines of the subway tunnel as they raced toward the train, bumping more than one commuter out of the way. The platform hosted about three dozen train rail travelers who were staring into either their mobile phones or studying various kinds of reading material. None seemed to notice Alex and Sam's quick arrival. Sam glanced toward the empty tracks.

"Here." Alex pointed to the computerized train schedule on the nearby wall. The train was a few minutes from arriving. They swiftly searched for another way out and found none. Blending with the crowd deemed the only option. They chose a spot about midway between the subway and where the platform ended. A large group of blue-collar workers roughly their age stood in a huddle, a few tall enough for Sam to effectively hide amongst. Alex took out the French tabloid from her bag and mimicked the commuters while Sam leaned in over her shoulder. From behind them, the loud footsteps of the police echoed toward them. Relieved that the officers had not entirely made it onto the platform, they seized the moment to catch their breath. When a young construction worker stepped forward and created a large space, Alex and Sam were forced to shuffle closer in among the group. Their hearts pounded against their chests. Sam wiped a bead of sweat that trickled down the side of his brow. From the corner of his eye, he spotted the first policeman cautiously move between the commuters, a second one close on his heels. The platform vibrated beneath their feet, announcing the imminent arrival of the train. Twenty seconds later the train came to a slow halt in front of them and, as if one body with the small group, they stepped onto the train. Careful not to move through the passengers too quickly, they slowly pushed their way to the further most corner. Having not yet laid eyes on his fugitives, the first policeman stepped onto the train and used one of the seats to stand on, affording him a better view over the passengers. Sam turned his back toward the law enforcement officer, turned Alex to face him and fervently kissed her until the train's doors finally shut behind them. They briefly paused, hovering in their romantic embrace while assessing if the policeman was still on the train. Much to their relief, as the train slowly rolled off, Sam spotted both policemen in a dazed and confused state on the platform.

The train made a multitude of small stops en route to the city and, using the route map displayed inside the train, Alex and Sam quickly knew which station to get off at. It was a few stations away from the train's final destination which played in their favor since they assumed that the police would in all likelihood be waiting for them at the final stop. According to the address Alex had found on the internet, the reporter's apartment was situated in an eastern commune about six miles from the Paris city center. When they arrived at the *Mairie des Lilas* train station, they disembarked onto a small, much quieter platform. Pleased that there was no sign of any police or men in suits waiting for them, they made their way through the subway into the streets. Several bakeries and coffee shops lined the cobbled road to where it stopped at a large fountain. Several food vendors traced the edges of the small village square sending an array of delicious smells past them.

Nearby, a street vendor's mobile food trolley cast blue flames and grey smoke into the air as he roasted the traditional chestnuts over an open fire and Alex briefly stopped to ask him for directions. It was a short walk through the park to where they found the old apartment building just as the vendor had directed. The building didn't look like much with patches of paint that peeled from the walls. The small strip of grass leading to the entrance was practically non-existent, and the glass in the entrance door hadn't been cleaned in what looked like decades. Sam pushed the number on the intercom, discovering it wasn't working. He tugged at the door handle to find, much to his surprise, that the door was unlocked. As they entered the small dingy foyer, Alex moved to where fifteen mailboxes were fixed to a dirty lilac wall. Matching the building's evident neglect several boxes' apartment numbers were too faded to read. Apart from the flight of stairs, the small entranceway was empty.

"Looks like we're taking the stairs," Sam said, as he gazed up into the stairwell.

Stopping on each floor, they quickly concluded that the reporter's apartment was situated on the top floor and proceeded to climb the multitude of steps to the fifth and final floor.

"I'm getting too old for this," Sam puffed when they finally reached the top.

"Really? Thirty-two is too old for you? It's all that food you're consuming," Alex joked back as she too had to stop briefly to catch her breath.

Apartment 527 was situated in the corner furthest away from the stairs. Alex gently tapped the rusted door knocker on the distressed blue wooden door. Her heartbeat accelerated when she heard the safety chain slip onto the door, followed by three more locks. A pair of green-brown eyes framed beneath heavy dark eyebrows peered at them through the small opening in the door.

"Oui?"

"Are you Gabriel Duval, the reporter from *La Découverte*?" Alex inquired in poor French.

The man replied in English.

"Who's asking?"

"I'm Alex, and this is Sam. We'd like to ask you a few questions about an article you wrote about a year ago."

"Which one?"

"The one about The Resistance."

The man slammed the door shut in their faces and made no further attempt to release the safety chain. Stunned, Alex reached for the door knocker again, but before she had a chance to use it, the green-brown eyes appeared again.

"Who are you?"

"I'm Alex and—"

"No! Who are you really?"

It was Sam who spoke next, "We believe they're trying to kill us."

"We need your help," Alex added.

The man's heavy eyebrows lowered even further before he closed the door and slid the safety chain off to invite them in.

"I wasn't expecting any guests," Gabriel said with a sheepish tone while he cleared empty pizza boxes off the only couch in the small open-plan room. The studio apartment was small and sparsely furnished. A large bookshelf divided the unmade bed from the rest of the tiny space. Apart from the excuse for a kitchenette opposite the bed, there was a desk squashed in the corner next to the bookshelf. The only wall shouldering the make-shift office was entirely covered in newspaper clippings, French phrases, a few black and white photos of men and a map with an assortment of yellow and black thumbtacks all over it. Alex turned and walked across the uneven squeaky wooden floor, pausing in front of the wall to take it all in.

"What can I do for you?" Gabriel spoke grumpily from the other end of the room, drawing her attention back to him and away from the information on the wall.

For the first time, Alex noticed his artificial leg—her eyes lingering on the titanium instrument a tad too long. Sam cleared his throat, nudging her in doing so.

"Sorry, I wasn't expecting—" Alex paused but then continued, "I saw the article you wrote in your magazine. I'm not that fluent in French, so I didn't quite understand it all, but we believe it's the same people who have been after us. To tell you the truth, they've been trying to kill us."

"I don't work for the magazine anymore." Gabriel pulled a sweater over his head and tossed a couple of empty red wine bottles into a waste bin in the kitchen. "How do you know it's The Resistance?"

"Well, we don't know for sure, which is why we're here." Sam spoke as he took a seat on the couch.

"Why are they after you?"

"We're not sure of that either."

"I can't help you. You should go."

Alex turned to face the wall, taking in the red rings drawn around a few names. "I think you can, Gabriel. You see, I recognize a few of these names on your wall."

Her comment seemed to have caught the closed-off reporter's attention. He uncrossed his arms and placed it on his hips.

"Who?"

"Jean-Pierre DuPont and Maurice d'Andigné."

The reporter's heavy eyebrows lifted in surprise.

"How do you know them?"

"Jean-Pierre DuPont is an industry colleague of mine at UNESCO, and the billionaire, Maurice d'Andigné, wrote me a letter requesting our help. We never got to meet him. They killed him and framed us for his murder. Now the police are after us too."

A few uneven steps had the now interested reporter next to her staring at the names on his wall. He remained silent, and then, as if his body was taken over by an entirely different person, his suspicious closed-off demeanor turned into effervescent excitement. He stretched across his desk and pulled a notebook and pen from underneath a pile of loose papers and notepads and hurriedly made his way to the couch.

"I'll help you, but I need to know everything. You don't mess with these people. Their authority reaches far beyond the borders of France. We're going to have to be very careful. They did this to me, you know? Bastards! My career is over thanks to them. All I'm good for now is writing food blogs for the local newspaper."

CHAPTER SIXTEEN

Gabriel Duval secured the locks on his apartment door and then hobbled to the only window in the room. He parted the yellowed voile curtain with two fingers, allowing a small gap that he peered through down into the street.

"Does anyone know you're here? Have you been followed?"

"No, we lost them before we boarded the train to come here."

"Good, we're going to have to make sure we're prepared for them." Gabriel took two strides into his kitchen, took a 9mm pistol from a cookie jar, checked the clip, and stuck it into his waistband. Taking a seat on the couch, he extended his titanium limb to one side. "Do you have any defense skills?"

Alex nodded, confirmed by Sam as he emptied their ample arsenal on the coffee table. Gabriel whistled, impressed by the unexpected weaponry his guests carried.

"We were also trained by British Special Forces."

"That covers it then," Gabriel said, pausing briefly before frowning. "Thought you said you worked for UNESCO?"

"With them, not for them. We're archaeologists, well actually, Sam's head of the archaeology faculty at Cambridge and I've since opened my own antiquities recovery firm. A recent mission had us working with DuPont."

"I see, and you say d'Andigné sent you a letter requesting your help."

"Correct, a series of letters actually. He brought us to Paris and the next thing we knew both he and his driver were dead."

"What did he need your help with?"

Alex had no way of knowing if Gabriel was trustworthy, but her instincts said he was. As it happened, there was little else they could do and no one else to trust.

"We're not certain, but it has something to do with this," she said, reaching into her bag.

Gabriel fixed his eyes on the encased organ on his coffee table then shook his shoulders and winced as if a spider had just crawled down his shirt.

"What is that thing?"

"A human heart. Actually, a two hundred and twenty-four-year-old heart of the once heir to the French throne," Sam informed the squeamish reporter.

"That's the most disgusting thing I've ever heard of. Where do you even find something like this?"

"It was hidden in d'Andigné's office." Alex took the confession letter from the base. "Then we found this letter. DuPont said it was a confession of some sorts just before he tried to murder us for it."

"You took it to DuPont? He knows about this?" Gabriel said agitated as he messed up his hair again.

"It's not like we had anyone else to go to. Who knew the man was twisted?" Sam defended.

"All we know is that the guys who tried to kill us all carried these." Alex placed the brass pawns on the table in front of him and then continued. "Both DuPont and d'Andigné wore signet rings with the emblem of a particular chess piece—DuPont had the knight and d'Andigné had the bishop. We suspect it's linked somehow. Can't be a coincidence."

Gabriel threw his notebook across the table and, with one arm loosely draped over his knee, stared at the chess pieces on his coffee table. "Do you know how many years I've been trying to get my hands on one of these?"

Sam glanced at Alex and then sideways to Gabriel. "Why, what are they?"

"These, my friends, are our way in." Gabriel fell back on his couch and expelled a jubilant cheer before jumping to his feet. He rubbed his hands through his already messy hair while he paced to his intel wall. With his fingers locked behind his neck, he stared into a faceless photo and muttered something in French under his breath.

"Duval, care to tell us what you're so ecstatic about?" Sam, who now sat on the edge of the couch, said with irritation.

Gabriel swung around, a smile so big it was hard to believe he was the same miserable guy who'd opened the door a mere twenty minutes ago. "You really don't know."

"Know what?" Alex asked, shoving the chess pieces back into her pocket.

"These are the keys to their headquarters. The keys!" He cheered again throwing his hands in the air. "I can't believe it. The day has finally come."

And as suddenly as his triumphant celebration had surprised Alex and Sam, Gabriel's personality just as quickly changed back to the paranoid reporter from before. He dashed to his desk and rummaged through the loose papers, flicking several pages to the floor. Alex and Sam could do nothing but wait and hope that their new colleague's sanity would return.

"Found it," he said, waving a paper above his head and then pinning it to his wall. "See this? That's the blueprint of *La Conciergerie,* at least as far as it can be proven."

Alex and Sam stood by his side, trying to make sense of the paper he'd stuck to the wall. It was a poor photocopy displaying a diagram of rooms and tunnels.

"Why are we looking at this?" Sam questioned. "Looks like a child drew it."

"It's where they meet, the headquarters of The Resistance. And now, because you have the keys, we can get inside."

"And do what?" Alex said, confused.

"What do you mean, do what? I'm going to give this guy what he deserves. I finally have my chance to put a bullet through both his legs."

"Not going to happen, Duval. That's not our fight to fight."

"I don't see you trying to get through life without a limb, Sam. I lost my wife, my kids, and everything I've worked for. It's payback time."

"So you're going to shoot the guy's legs off. That's ridiculous!" Sam retorted.

Gabriel pulled his gun from his waist and pointed it at Sam's leg. "Okay tough guy, let's see if you can handle being without a leg. I bet you won't sing the same tune then, buddy."

"All right, boys, calm down! Gabriel put the gun down. We didn't come here for this," Alex spoke sternly. "I said, put your gun down, Gabriel!"

He finally did as he was told and lowered his gun, all the while keeping his gaze fixed on Sam.

"I get that you want to take revenge on the guy, but there's a lot more we can do to bring him and everyone that's in The Resistance down. They're hiding something. Something huge, and my gut tells me they've done a lot more than take your leg. You can get your life back, Gabriel. Think about it. If we do this the right way, you won't go down as a disgruntled victim who sought revenge. You'd be the investigative reporter responsible for the biggest exposé the world has ever seen! Instead of being locked up in a prison cell, your name would be written in the history books. Every tabloid in Europe, heck the world, would want you."

Alex watched as Gabriel took her words in and then shuffled to his kitchen to open a bottle of wine. She was right, and he knew it. He pulled three paper cups from a dusty cupboard and filled each with some wine.

"Fine, what do you suggest?" he said, plonking the cups down in front of them.

Sam took a large swig of his wine then lightly pressed his

cup to Gabriel's. "Don't ever point a gun at me again, got it? I'm not here to make enemies," he said, gesturing for him to accept the toast.

"Sorry, I get carried away sometimes."

"Can we leave the bromance for another time and come up with a strategy, please boys?" Alex spoke over her shoulder as she walked to the intel wall. "How do you know they meet at *La Conciergerie*?"

"I knew a guy on the inside. He's dead now. They killed him."

"And he drew this?" Alex referred to the sketch.

"Yes."

"Can we get our hands on a better one?"

"It wouldn't help. The blueprints registered with the council don't include what's underground."

"So you're saying these tunnels are underground," Sam queried, to which Gabriel nodded.

"And your friend, he walked these tunnels."

"Yes, he was part of The Resistance."

"How do you become a member?"

"You don't. It gets passed on through the family. If your father or uncle was one, then you inherit the right to join. The males only, that is."

"Do we know how far they go back? What do they stand for?" Sam asked again.

"As far as I know it dates back to the French Revolution when an elite of wealthy commoners, mostly manufacturers, professionals, and merchants, formed a social order who aspired to political power. It is said that they were extremely influential and largely to blame for the overthrow of the monarchy. Over time their membership grew, spreading across the world, and with it, their influence. And yes, before you ask, no one knows for sure who the members are but, over the years many of the names associated with them have been heads of corporations, senior government officials, Supreme Court justices, and even presidents. I've heard so many theories as to what their motives are but the ones that seem to stick the most range from controlling the Central Intelligence Agency, belonging to a global network aimed at world domination and even being part of the Illuminati."

Alex and Sam fell quiet.

"Told you these guys aren't to be messed with."

"So you're saying they use these chess pieces to gain access to *La Conciergerie*."

"Each member has a chess piece. Depending on your hierarchy, you get anything from a pawn to a knight and a bishop. I'm assuming the queen would belong to the highest-ranking member." Gabriel's knuckles whitened against the wine bottle in his hand.

"And the rings? Do all of them wear a ring, like a rank or something?" Sam asked, trying to distract Gabriel from his anger.

"That I don't know. It's the first I've heard of the rings, but hey, seems appropriate."

Alex paced the tiny room, eventually pausing in front of the heart. "I just don't understand where this heart fits in."

"Maybe it doesn't. You said you found it in d'Andigné's house. He was an art collector. Could just be a valuable piece he decided to hide."

"No, I don't think so. DuPont was pretty stuck on wanting it."

"Yeah, so stuck he was prepared to kill us for it," Sam added.

"Can you see if you can perhaps make out what this letter's about? My French language skills don't extend to the antiquated eighteenth century's. It's also full of squiggles and blotches."

She passed the handwritten letter to Gabriel, who seemed to take his time with it. Alex tapped her fingers on the side of her paper cup. When Gabriel finally lifted his head, he topped up his paper cup and threw back the red liquid without saying a word.

"And? What does it say?" Alex pushed impatiently for an answer.

"It's the ramblings of a mad man if you ask me. Can't make heads or tails of it."

"Why not? You're French. Surely you can understand something," Sam added, annoyed with the man.

"I'm telling you what I know, okay. I can't understand it. The French used extremely complicated phrases back then, and it's more like poetry and parables than straightforward writing. Besides, I'm only half French. My mother was an American."

"That explains why you're fluent, then. Still doesn't help us with the letter," Alex said, placing it back into the hidden pouch.

"I might know a guy who can help with that, though. He used to be one of my contacts. I haven't seen him since, well, since I lost my leg and all, but I can try to make contact with him again."

"Can you trust him?"

"He saved my life. If it weren't for him, I'd have been six feet under the ground."

"Fine, how do we find him?" Alex said while securing a gun in the small of her back and another in her waistband in the front.

"*We* don't. I will. You two stay put until I get back, and stay low. There's still some of my ex-wife's clothes under the bed, and I might have something for you in there too, from before I lost all the extra pounds."

As Gabriel Duval shut the door behind him, Sam turned to Alex. "Think we can trust him?"

"I'll shoot his other leg off myself if he crosses us."

G abriel eventually returned to his apartment some three hours later.

"Where have you been, Duval? How long does it take to find someone?"

"Hey, I haven't seen him in almost five years. It's not that easy to find someone who's in hiding."

"But you did, right?" Alex came between the men who were at it again.

"Of course. Turns out he was right where one would expect to find him. We're meeting him in ninety minutes."

Alex had slipped into black leather pants and a matching black leather jacket that belonged to his ex-wife. Gabriel's eyes settled in a forlorn look on her attire, and Alex was confident she spotted tears in his eyes. "I'll return it," she said gently.

"No need, she's gone for good."

CHAPTER SEVENTEEN

An hour later the trio stepped out onto the *Richelieu* station's platform in the center of Paris. It was close to ten pm and apart from a handful of young adults waiting for the last train out, the station was quiet and somewhat eerie. Out in the streets, weekend socialites roamed in and out of busy street clubs. Restaurants and take out shops were equally lively while the last of the clothing boutiques had shut down for the night. They turned into a narrow street between tall buildings. Lined with scaffolding on the one side and rows of bicycle stands on the other, there were hardly any streetlights. Loud music from a noisy bar with a bright red door had a line of at least fifty youths waiting for entry on the sidewalk.

"Where are we meeting this guy?" Sam asked when a small gang of bikers sped by.

Gabriel ignored his question, and instead told them to wait

outside a large semi-modern building. Alex read the sign on the building. "Bibliothèque Nationale de France; says here it closed two hours ago. Why would he bring us to the national library when it's closed? Surely he's not expecting us to meet the guy out here in public?" Alex felt uneasy. Her hand rested under her jacket on the gun in her back.

Sam pushed his chin out as Gabriel beckoned for them to meet him where he was standing twenty feet away. When they reached him, Alex curled her fingers around her gun's handle and settled her index finger just above the trigger.

"No need, it's safe. Come with me." Gabriel put them at ease and led them down a short steel stairwell one would hardly know was there if you didn't go looking for it. When they reached the bottom, he knocked twice on a matching black steel door. Sam cast a watchful eye over their surroundings but was given little time to do so before the door flung open. A short man, roughly in his late sixties, opened the door and invited them inside and down a cold dark passage. The corridor's walls were a total contradiction to that of the building outside in that it was entirely made from stone dating back to at least the fifteenth century. At the end of the seemingly endless dark corridor, it opened up into a sizeable tidy room with marble floors and row upon row of card catalogs. They weaved their way through the tall steel shelving and finally entered a room roughly the size of Gabriel's apartment. But unlike his messy bachelor pad, this one was warm and neat as a pin.

"Francois, meet my friends Alex and Sam," Gabriel offered a brief introduction. The man's friendly, almost exuberant response surprised both Alex and Sam, resembling that of a grandparent rather than a secret contact.

"So, my friend Gabriel tells me you need my help with a document."

Alex lifted the artifact from the backpack and followed the usual sequence to retrieving the ancient letter.

"Don't ask, Francois. Trust me, you're better off not looking at that up close," Gabriel offered when his friend looked at the heart with intrigue.

He bellowed a warm laugh and carefully unfolded the letter on a nearby desk, shining a tiny green lamp on both it and the shiny bald patch on the crown of his head. Squinting through his reading glasses' thick lenses, Francois slowly ran his eyes line for line over the letter. About midway through the letter, Francois paused and looked directly at Alex and Sam before continuing. Alex bit a piece of rough skin from the side of her thumb. Without words, she exchanged thoughts with Sam, concluding that he must have found something significant to warrant that glance.

When Francois eventually finished, he switched off the desk lamp and sat staring at the letter in complete silence. It took just about everything for Alex to not ask him the burning question that clearly he had trouble conveying. When he finally took his reading glasses off and fiddled with them in his hands, he looked pensively at Sam and Alex.

"Are you sure you are ready for this?"

After exchanging silent words of agreement, they both nodded in reply.

Francois placed his glasses back on his face and folded his hands in his lap. "The author of this letter introduces himself as *R.J. Pinoir II*, the son of *R.J. Pinoir I,* who was the medical practitioner responsible for the autopsy on a ten-year-old boy called Louis Charles de France. He goes on to say he was the surviving child of King Louis XVI and Marie Antoinette and had become the unclaimed King of France upon their death." Francois paused and glanced with caution at his friend.

"We know that part Francois, what else," Alex nudged gently.

"He makes mention of a movement." Francois jumped to his feet and started pacing the room. "I don't think this is wise. We should burn it and forget we ever saw it."

Stunned, Alex stopped Francois in the middle of the room. "We're not going to burn it, Francois. We're in too deep. It's our only way out of a mess we unwillingly got dragged into. You need to tell us the rest."

"You have no idea who you are involved with, Alex. This movement has control beyond this city you find yourself in. They have the power to destroy your life—all of our lives! It's taken me many years hiding in this hole to get the target off my back." He turned to Gabriel. "You shouldn't have brought them here."

"Francois, my friend, this is our opportunity. These two are our best chance of wiping them out once and for all. You and I, we have nothing left to lose. Apart from the miserable lives we're clinging onto we've already lost everything we once loved. I want my life back. I'm tired of letting them get away with it." Gabriel shuffled over to his friend and placed his hands on his friend's shoulders. "Do it for Angelique. You have a chance to prove that you're not the insane old man she believes her father to be. You still have her. You can win her back."

The cozy room fell silent as Alex and Sam watched the two men's despairing exchange. They shared a mutual bond that ran so deep with loss and sorrow that it was hard not to be moved by it.

Alex took Francois' hand. "I'm sorry we involved you in this. I promise your name will not be mentioned when we leave here tonight. We will defend you and ourselves and expose The Resistance for who they are, I give you my word."

Something in Alex's eyes conveyed the truth, and a compassion Francois knew was sincere. He wiped his wet eyes with the cuff of his moss-green cardigan and took a seat behind the desk again. Taking a deep breath, he continued.

"*Pinoir* mentions the movement which calls itself *La Résistance* whose sole aim it was to destroy the French monarchy and dominate the world. He talks about how they conspired against the monarchy and ordered the Bastille invasion as well as the King and Queen's executions. Then he talks about the boy, the dauphin, who they tortured, starved and held a prisoner in the Temple fortress hoping he would die naturally, except he didn't. Instead, the boy escaped, and no one ever saw him again. They couldn't let the people find out the truth, so they killed the boy's doctor and bribed the local doctor, the writer's father, *R.J. Pinoir* I. He says they threatened to kill his family if his father didn't help them. So he did as he was told and stole the corpse of the first dauphin, Louis Joseph who died of natural causes in June of 1789. He was ten, so his heart matched the size of his brother's. They defrauded the people of France by fabricating the dauphin's death to destroy what was left of the monarchy."

Francois placed his reading glasses on the letter and sat back in his chair, staring at the floor. "The entire Republic is nothing but a lie. All fabricated and coerced into existence."

"That will explain why these people have been hunting us down. If the world knew their secret, they would come down like a house of cards. All their influence and control throughout the world would disappear. For more than two centuries they've deceived the people into thinking the monarchy had died during the Revolution. Heck, the entire

Revolution was nothing but a deception of epic proportions," Sam exclaimed.

Alex walked over to where the heart stood on the table. "D'Andigné was one of them. That's why he needed our help—to expose the truth. He knew this was the single most important evidence, and all that was needed to bring them down. That's why he had my underfloor safety box installed —because he knew I'd find his. He risked everything and paid with his life to get this to us."

"And that's why DuPont was so eager to get his hands on it too. Except he wanted to make sure the secret stayed locked and buried forever," Sam added.

"We can't risk anyone discovering this heart or the letter. We have to hide it somewhere safe," Alex cautioned while placing the letter back in its base and securing it in their backpack.

"You have to take it with you, I can't keep it here," Francois declared, waving his wrinkled hands in front of his face.

"My place isn't safe either," Gabriel added.

"I think I know exactly where it will be the safest and have the most impact when it is rediscovered," Sam said with a smug smile on his face.

"You're right," Alex agreed as if he had declared his thoughts out loud.

"Where?" Gabriel pushed, annoyed at how his new friends seemed to know each other's thoughts.

"Best you don't know, Gabriel. For your own protection."

"And if something happened to the two of you? Your secret hiding place would die with you."

"You're a clever man, Duval. I'm sure you'd figure it out eventually. Besides, we don't plan on getting killed," Sam assured him.

"Fine, then what, you hide the heart and then? How do we bring them down? I'm not letting go of this. You promised me we'd expose them."

"Calm down, Duval. We're not going to break our promise to you. We have every intention of unveiling The Resistance and every single secret, crime and lie we can lay our hands on."

"Care to share our plan and when we intend to execute it?"

"No-no, you're not coming with us. It's too dangerous. Not to offend you, but I'm not sure how fast you can run. And it will come to that. We need you here."

Gabriel sat on the small brown couch, extending his artificial leg as he always did. "Stupid leg, they've stolen my revenge too."

"You'll have your moment of revenge, Gabriel. Shooting a

man isn't the answer. In our line of business, we've learned to use intellect instead. Be patient," Alex reassured him.

"Now, Francois, I realize it might be too much to ask of you, but this place makes for the best option to use as our base." Alex paused as she gave their host time to reflect.

Francois simply nodded in agreement and turned to put the kettle on.

"Thank you. We won't compromise your safety. If all goes well, we should be back here in an hour, and then we can run through our plan. For now, we need to get this to safety. Gabriel, we're going to need those blueprints and any information you have on when The Resistance's next meeting is, the protocol and how to gain entry. Make sure you get it right. There's no room for error. If we get one detail wrong, the mission fails and we all get killed. Don't trust anyone, do you hear me? No one! We will meet you back here in an hour. Francois, we'll knock twice, pause and then knock three more times on the door."

And with that, Alex and Sam left and disappeared into the darkness of the Paris night.

CHAPTER EIGHTEEN

The map borrowed from Francois' underground abode led them to the nearest bus stop not far from their current location. From there it would be a fifteen-minute bus ride and a short walk to where Maurice d'Andigné's apartment was near the *Arc de Triomphe.* They walked briskly, keeping an eye on anything out of sorts. Nearing the bus stop, they suspected they were being followed and ducked into the enclave of a closed grocery shop. With their guns in hand, they pinned their backs to the wall and waited for the suspect to approach. When the black-hooded man walked past without any reaction, they fell in behind him to where he eventually entered a quiet apartment block opposite the bus stop. At ease, Alex and Sam stepped onto the bus. Inside the lights were on, illuminating only a few passengers—a couple in full embrace in the back of the bus, a small group of socialites and two more men who also got on and took their seats toward the middle of the bus behind each other. Making provisions for a quick exit, Alex and Sam sat in the first seats on either side of the aisle behind the bus driver. Sam turned sideways in his seat, with his back pinned against the window, while Alex kept her eye on the bus driver's rear-view mirror that afforded a view of all the passengers behind her.

The bus pulled away and made its way toward the 8th arrondissement of Paris. The streets were much quieter than earlier, and it was hard not to be mesmerized by all Paris had to offer. When they got off at their arrival stop, Sam noticed two men getting off using the second door at the back of the bus. He silently alerted Alex, who had seen it too. Continuing with their silent communications, Alex and Sam reverted to what they were trained to do in these situations and split up where the *Arc de Triomphe* was directly in front of them, and the road circled it. They remained alert as they walked in opposite directions from each other along the quiet road around the monument. As predicted, the two men split up too—one behind Alex and one behind Sam. Their suspicions were further confirmed when Alex and Sam once again tested their pursuit and walked toward the open square positioned around the historic building. Again, both men did the same. Alex increased her pace as she approached the large arch. So did her stalker. Until now, she only had her hand close to her gun, but as she neared the structure, she pulled her firearm from her waistband and placed her finger on the trigger. Her eyes searched for Sam but turned up empty. Behind her, she heard her stalker's footsteps quicken. Her free hand tightened each of the backpack's straps, securing it closer to her body. A few yards and she'd use the arched structure to hide behind. She increased her pace too, still searching for Sam, who was nowhere to be seen. Resolving that he'd be fine on his own, she placed her focus on her enemy. When she reached the building, she hid behind the square column. Operating on instinct and adrenaline alone, she waited for the man to make his move. And, as expected, he did. Her arm blocked his powerful punch, catching him off guard. He swung his other fist, narrowly missing the side of her face. His foot thrust a powerful blow to her knee, and she fell to the ground. Overestimating that he had won the fight already, he took too long to deliver his next blow, and Alex caught his arm and twisted it securely into her armpit. Back on her feet, she rotated his body, forcing his arm against his elbow's bend. The man cringed with pain when she lifted his arm higher, inflicting even more injury to his shoulder joint.

"Who are you and who are you working for?"

The man didn't answer. Placing more force on his arm, she asked again, but the result was the same. Her thoughts trailed to Sam. Deciding they had to get on with their mission, she slammed the back of her pistol against her stalker's head, yielding him unconscious at her feet.

She hid behind the concrete structure and listened for any clue to indicate Sam's position. She knew he had to be nearby. In the distance she heard groaning and a split second later, the dull, muffled sound of a gun discharging through a silencer numbed her body with fear. She ran toward the direction it had come from and saw two male figures on the ground. With her gun pointed and aimed at them, she approached with vigilance. As she neared, she saw Sam flat on his back with his stalker's body spread diagonally across his torso. She kept her gun on the man's back.

"Sam! Get up, Sam!" Panic restricted her breathing in her throat as she watched her fiancée and partner lie dead still on the ground. She kicked the man's feet, discovering them to be flaccid. He didn't respond. She went down on one knee and kept her gun firm against the attacker's back while, with her other hand, she gently tapped Sam's cheek.

"Get this imbecile off me," Sam groaned as he attempted to move out from under his victim.

"Are you shot?"

"Not that I know of, but he is."

Alex pushed the man off with her foot. He rolled onto his back to reveal the sizeable self-inflicted bullet wound in his abdomen. With his gun still in his hand, it was clear the two had had a struggle, and the gun had gone off.

"Are you sure you're okay?" she asked Sam again as she helped him to his feet.

"Certain. That was a close call though. Where's your guy?"

"Unconscious, over there. We need to get out of here. We don't have much time."

Relieved that they had both escaped unscathed, they entered Maurice d'Andignè's apartment less than five minutes later.

T he apartment was dark and unoccupied. Fingerprint powder lay scattered on just about every door, surface, and windowsill throughout the apartment. Up in the office, his corpse had been removed and the scene was pretty much as they had left it. Comforted by the fact that the police hadn't discovered the underfloor safe, they carefully replaced the artifact in its original place of safety and rolled the carpet back in place.

"Let's get back to HQ," Sam urged, but Alex ignored him. She was standing stationary behind d'Andigné's desk, taking in every angle of the room.

"I know that look, what's brewing?"

"I just thought if d'Andigné was one of them, and he had the bishop emblem in his ring, then he was pretty influential in the hierarchy."

"I suppose. Why?"

"Don't you think he'd have some other kind of evidence, like a dossier with all the member's names?"

Sam grew quiet as he reflected on her words.

"They did take his computer, so I would say that the theory might be very accurate. I doubt something that powerful would have a paper trail. It would be encrypted or pass-word-protected at the very least. It entirely explains why they took his computer."

"You're right. Assuming that's accurate, it would mean that the original file would be at *La Conciergerie*. We have to get our hands on that list."

When they reached the front door, Sam trailed off toward the garage.

"Where are you going? We have to get out of here, Sam."

"You didn't think we were going to take the bus back again, did you? Look what I found in his desk while you were playing Sherlock Holmes." Sam dangled a set of keys between his index finger and thumb, smiling as if he had just won a prize. "Besides, it will be faster."

Sam was right when less than six minutes later, they parked d'Andigné's Mercedes SL500 in an underground parking lot about a block away and delivered the coded knock on their newly established headquarters' black steel door. Angst overcame them when, after having to repeat their coded knock, Francois still didn't open. It was only after the third attempt that he opened the door, looking anxious and far less effervescent than when they first met him.

"What's wrong?" Alex asked.

"Gabriel's not come back yet. He should've been here already."

Sam glimpsed at his watch. "It's only just gone sixty minutes. I'm sure he'll be back any minute now."

But Sam's attempt at putting Francois at ease had little effect on the man.

"Why don't you get some rest? I'll make you a cup of tea," Alex offered, already popping on the kettle. But much to their joy, the kettle hadn't even reached a slow boil when they heard the coded rap on the door. Gabriel limped more than usual down the long corridor.

"Are you okay?" Sam enquired when he noticed Gabriel dragging his false leg.

"I'll be fine, just all this walking tonight. I'm not used to it anymore." He hated to admit it, confirming their reasons for him staying behind even further.

"We couldn't do this if you weren't helping us from this end," Sam said with an empathetic tone as if he knew the contempt Gabriel felt in the moment.

When they reached Alex and Francois in his quarters, Gabriel's voice took on a more upbeat tone, resolved to his mission being from behind the desk. "I brought a couple of extra gadgets I thought we'd need." He emptied his back-pack on the coffee table. "Thought these in-ear mics might come in handy. They're undetectable at first glance and have a two-mile radius connecting to my laptop. It's not the latest in spyware, but it should do the trick. I also figured we could record a bit of extra footage in support of our case file. Looks like a button but it's a camera. Neat, huh?"

Gabriel's enthusiasm over his small supply of spy equip-ment was a joy to watch, making it more than evident that the mission excited him and that he was eager to get back into the game.

"Oh and this is my *pièce de résistance,* no pun intended," he chuckled, waving what looked like an ordinary flash drive in the air. "It's a two-in-one flash drive that not only decrypts just about any code but also copies it within thirty seconds. Just insert into the device, and it does it for you."

"I thought you said we're looking for a physical ledger. Doubt we'd need to use the flash drive," Alex commented.

"And I'm not even going to ask where you got all this stuff, my friend," Sam spoke while inspecting the gadgets up close.

"Well, if you're an investigative reporter this is par for the course. Got it from a Russian contact of mine. We go way back. Anyway, what's the plan?"

"Do you have the blueprints?"

Gabriel fixed his hand drawn map to the wall. "I have more than a blueprint, my friends. I have undercover recordings, dates, events schedules, you name it, an entire file made possible by my contact, may he rest in peace."

O ver the following twelve hours, the newly assembled team researched and studied every inch of The Resistance's meeting place at *La Conciergerie* and their assembly sequence along with all the information Gabriel had in his possession. With access to the national library situated on the floor above them, they managed to trace historical events and fraudulent documents, confirming what little known facts existed about the clandestine exploits The Resistance had been associated with over the past two decades. A methodically constructed covert operation to locate and retrieve the dossier with members' names was formulated and rehearsed down to the finest detail.

Wearing the ear mics, Sam would pose as a member, carrying one of the pawns to gain entry to the meeting. Guided from their headquarters, Gabriel would talk him through the sequence of events, and aid in navigating the tunnels all while Sam was recording whatever footage was available through his secret camera. Alex would be positioned in a small antechamber next to one of the prison cells, waiting for Sam's signal to access the underground tunnels that would lead to an office. According to their intel, there would be a vault containing the dossier. Once they had it, Alex would return with it to her secret hideout until daylight and escape the same way she'd entered—posing as a tourist. Sam would return to the meeting and leave as if nothing happened. Their plan was faultless.

"I think we're ready," Alex announced.

"Quite the odd twist of comedy that The Resistance will be exposed in the very place where they held their Revolutionary tribunals, and Marie Antoinette spent the last days of her life." It was Francois who spoke when he closed a thick history book he held in his hand. "To think, all these decades and centuries they were single-handedly responsible for bringing down the French monarchy and instigating the entire Revolution. France's very own people. They're a disgrace to our country."

"Let's get some rest boys. We're going to need it tomorrow night. We'll do a quick run-through again before we deploy, but I think we've got it," Alex said.

CHAPTER NINETEEN

"You clean up nice for an archaeologist, Sam," Gabriel mocked when Sam stepped out in the black tailcoat and top hat Gabriel had discovered amongst his late informant's belongings. "I always thought being an archaeologist was boring, digging around in tombs all day. But you two make it look much more exciting."

Sam chuckled. "If only, mate! Truth be told, our careers have veered far off the track of late. Each time we get plunged into a mission, we never know if we'll come out alive. You'll be surprised how much evil there is in the world."

"Money has always been the root of all evil, my friends. Power, greed, and money—the evil tri-factor. Since the early days of man, it's ruled the world, and I'm not sure it will ever change," Francois added.

"Well, what do you boys say we deal with them one at a time, starting with The Resistance?"

"I'd say, there's never been a better day for that than today, my love. Let's go get them!" Sam cheered.

W hen the sun cast shadows long and wide across the city of Paris, the team deployed. Using D'Andignés luxury car, Sam looked every bit the part of the hidden movement's elite when he arrived at the historic building. He glanced at the clock on the car's console. It was 19:55, and he was right on schedule as planned.

"Testing, testing," Sam checked his earpiece.

"Receiving loud and clear, Sam. Alex?" Gabriel sent back.

"Copy that, HQ. In position," Alex responded from her tiny hiding place where she had gained access into the building just before they shut down the main admission area to the public at 1800 hours. She had sneaked inside the historic building taking on the part of a tourist and used the interactive guide-maps available to the public to navigate her way. Her position had her stationed in the small antechamber, which was once used as the grooming room, a place where prisoners had their hair cut before execution by guillotine. Being there alone in utter darkness was horrifying and ghostly and sent shivers down her spine.

Satisfied their comms were operational, Sam left the car

south of the River Seine from where they would make their escape. It was the only accessible route across the narrow bridge since the entire building was constructed on a small island in the middle of the river. When he approached the back of the monument, he reached for the brass pawn in his inside breast pocket. As researched, the low palisade gave way to a matching black cast iron pedestrian gate. He cast his eyes on the green door with its crisscross iron bars just inside the fence. A solid limestone staircase lined by sculptures built into the building's walls, ran above the green door; leading to another door slightly bigger in size. Over the door, the sculpted head of a lion protruded from the stair's railing, marking The Resistance's secret entrance.

Sam's heart pounded against his chest. They might have had intel from Gabriel's informant, but the facts were that any of the details could have been changed since he'd been killed almost five years before. His palm was clammy when he turned the gate's copper doorknob; twice to the right, four times to the left and ended with seven times to the right. Like a combination to a vault, the gate parted from the fence. He turned around and looked over his shoulder once more. Behind him, the small parking area was quiet. There wasn't a soul in sight. He moved toward the green door in front of him. The brass pawn figurine fitted perfectly into the slightest of indentations where the distressed double green wooden doors joined in the middle. Again he heard the click, making his heart surge with a new dose of adrenalin.

"Granted," he whispered.

"Copy that, Sam. Standing by," Alex whispered back.

Sam pushed the doors open and stepped inside a wide corridor with a domed roof. The walls were made from large limestone squares upon which small torches were mounted every few yards. It was unattended with no sign of surveillance cameras or anything similar. Sam's shiny black shoes echoed between the solid walls as he walked along the thirteenth-century structure. At the very end of the corridor, it ran dead at a wall equal in structure to the rest of the passageway. Again, Sam took his pawn and placed it in the center of the third limestone square from the right of the seventh row from the floor. The now-familiar click was heard again before the wall gave way to a narrow stairwell in which the staircase ran far steeper than he'd anticipated.

"Granted," he reported again.

"Copy that, Sam," Alex responded once again.

"You should descend into the small chamber first, Sam, then veer right toward the second chamber. I'm sure there'll be quite a few members already. The camera is recording," Gabriel affirmed.

So far, everything ran according to plan, but Sam couldn't help being anxious. He had no idea what to expect or worse, who to expect.

"I've got your back, Sam. Just use our safe word," Alex

whispered in his earpiece as if she sensed his trepidation. Sam didn't respond for fear of compromising their mission. He had now entered the larger chamber where a group of at least two hundred men in coat-tails and top hats were seated in chairs arranged in rows to form a horseshoe. At the open end of the U-shape, a distinguished man sat facing the members. With a striking resemblance to Abraham Lincoln, his authority was marked by the red satin sash that ran diagonally across his body. On it, an embroidered rook chess piece cemented his rank. To his right were two men, each wearing a blue rosette on their left shoulders, their rankings declared by a gold embroidered bishop.

Two raised viewing galleries flanked the U-shaped seating area where Sam took his seat in the back row of the east wing as planned. The night's proceedings hadn't commenced yet, and Sam listened to the murmuring ramblings of the men surrounding him. Conversations were taking place in several languages some of which he didn't recognize. From their intel, Sam knew the meeting was due to start any moment now. Directing his hidden camera toward the chamber, he captured several members' faces across the room. On his left sat a rather pompous man with neatly cut white hair and a matching thick white mustache that curled up at the ends. His face, in contrast to his white hair, was red and blotchy in places. He merely nodded as Sam shuffled impatiently in his seat.

"I always wish they would get on with these meetings too,"

he leaned in and whispered in a thick German accent at Sam. "Herr Lichtenstein III," he introduced himself.

Caught off guard Sam introduced himself in reply. "Lord Wedgewood," he said, quickly recalling the article his mother had once read on the creator of her Wedgewood fine china dinner service. "Do you come to all these meetings?" he asked before the stranger caught onto his deceit.

"Oh absolutely, Lord Wedgewood. It is critical to our existence that we execute our plans with great precision."

Somehow, Sam anticipated the man to be a stickler for discipline. "Which motion do you support most?"

"We have to get a grip on bitcoin, in my opinion. You?"

Relieved to hear the speaker call the meeting to order, Sam only nodded in response.

The Lincoln lookalike spoke in perfect English, his accent only vaguely recognizable as being French. Trailing his eyes across the large cavernous chamber, Sam recognized more than a handful of men. There were politicians, billionaires, oil magnates, and a vast array of incredibly influential people hailing from anywhere from Russia across to America—each sharing the same secret. He felt sick to his stomach as his thoughts wandered to the deceit and destruction this movement must have caused over all these centuries, unbeknownst to the regular man on the street.

The first motion on the table was called in to vote, and soon after, they announced a short recess to tally the ballots. Sam followed the small gathering of men through a door positioned behind each wing.

"Here's our gap, Sam. See the door to your far left? That will take you to the chambers behind the main hall," Gabriel spoke in Sam's ear.

Sam carefully moved through the group of men most of whom stood arguing over the motion's ruling, creating for the perfect distraction to aid his getaway. He paused a few yards from the door and turned around to face the men who were too busy debating to notice his position. He slowly backed into the door, turned around when he was a few feet away, and exited the debating room.

"I'm in," he announced.

On the other side of the door, the small dark passage led him fifty yards away to where it split into two. "Which way?" he prompted.

"Hold on," Gabriel answered back, "it's not on the blueprint. Are you sure you took the correct door?"

"Duval, you'd better not be messing with me. Of course, I'm sure, now which way?"

"I'm not, I swear. There's no mention of it. Pick either of them."

Annoyed, Sam took the left tunnel. The place sent chills down his spine. From their research, they knew these tunnels might have aided some prisoners to escape their fateful execution, many of whom never made it out. Strange sounds echoed behind him. He knew he was alone, but he couldn't shake the feeling that he had company. He wasn't one to believe in ghosts but every hair the back of his neck attested to the opposite.

"Duval, you'd better have found out where I am. I don't have much time, and this place is creeping me out."

"Sam," Alex's voice came over the airwaves, "check your direction, you should be heading in a north-western direction."

"Copy that," he said, clicking one of the buttons on his wristwatch, a high-tech survival gift Alex had given him for Christmas.

"North-west. Affirmative," he responded, slightly more at ease now that he appeared to have selected the correct tunnel.

"Got it!" Gabriel interjected. "You should hit a dead end up ahead. When you get to it, let me know."

Several quickened paces further, Sam reached the wall. "Now what?"

"It's not actually a wall. You need to figure out how to open it. There should be a small lever or something."

"Are you kidding me, Duval? There's nothing here. It's a blank wall."

"Sam, perform a sound test," Alex offered.

He responded by knocking on the bricks in several places. Each delivered a hollow response except one positioned in front of his left foot. Using his hand, he applied pressure to the block and heard a series of grinding noises before the wall parted in the corner to his right, creating a gap just big enough for him to slip through sideways; he squeezed through. Expecting another dark passage, he was surprised to have found his way into a kitchen.

"I'm in the kitchen."

"Copy that, coming down to meet you now," Alex announced.

Two minutes later, Alex joined him where he was inspecting a kitchen gadget the purpose of which was a mystery.

"Fancy meeting you here," he joked when Alex walked in. "Mind telling me what this contraption is?"

Alex giggled, "It's a paddle churn, for making butter, silly. Makes you appreciate the convenience of it now, doesn't it? Thought you'd never get here. This place is creepy."

"I know, I'm close to changing my opinion about ghosts. Could have sworn there was someone behind me back there."

"Shall we get on with it then so we can get out of here?"

"Thought you'd never ask."

"Gabriel, do you copy?"

"I copy loud and clear. Was waiting for you two to stop rambling."

"Which way is the vault, Duval?"

"You need to go back through the secret door then take the left fork about fifty yards in."

Alex and Sam slipped back through the secret door, closing it behind them by activating it the same way it opened. Gabriel's intel was correct and fifty-two yards on further on, they reached the fork and veered left. Now grateful for Alex's small flashlight, it was slightly less daunting as the pair navigated their way through the dark underground tunnel. The tunnel was substantially shorter, and it wasn't long after that they found the ladder attached to the wall in the middle of the tunnel as was laid out on the blueprint.

"Found the ladder, Duval," Alex said, forgetting that the flashlight now afforded Gabriel a better view through the secret camera.

"The button should be on the side next to the eighth step," Gabriel followed through.

"Copy that," Alex responded as she ascended the ladder. Her fingers found the button and, upon pushing it, she heard the practically inaudible popping noise above their heads as the latch opened. Alex switched off the flashlight and peered through the narrow gap into a well-lit room. By their account, the room should be the private office Gabriel's informant had said belonged to The Resistance. She slowly raised the hatch with her head, all the while keeping her eyes scanning the room for any occupants. The lights were on which might have meant there was someone there. Much to her relief, it was vacant. She lifted the top half of her body through the narrow floor opening which was positioned behind a sizeable mahogany desk. Caught waist-high in the hatch, she heard the door open revealing two male voices.

CHAPTER TWENTY

Alex crouched down beneath the floor and rapidly slid the panel back in place above her head. They paused, hovering on the ladder in total darkness while listening to the subdued voices above their heads.

"What's happening?" Gabriel nudged through their earpieces.

They ignored him, in fear of compromising themselves. Gabriel repeatedly pushed for answers.

"Quiet!" Alex finally whispered back, praying she wasn't heard. From the office above, the men's footsteps moved away from the desk directly above their heads. They listened as the door opened and then closed. Alex remained in position, waiting, listening for any sounds.

"I think they've left," Sam whispered.

"I can't be sure I heard both leave, assuming we actually only heard two of them. There might have been more, who knows?"

"We don't, but we're going to need to risk it and hope for the best."

Deciding to trust Sam's advice, Alex pushed the button on the side of the ladder. The popping sound followed. Her hand reached for her gun, just in case. Eased by the lack of any sounds or movement in the room, she cautiously slid the hatch aside. There was no one there, so she continued into the room.

"Clear," she whispered indicating to Sam to climb up too, briefly pausing on the spot.

Alex took in the room from behind the mahogany desk where it stood a few yards away from the wall behind her. Next to her, a paired brown leather chair with brass claw feet had been neatly tucked in behind the desk. Apart from the blue leather binder on the desk, the surface was clear. She skimmed the corners of the room in search of security cameras just as Sam took his place next to her. Her search came up empty. To their right, heavy blue drapes covered the only window in the room, and to their left, the entire wall was taken up by an impressive collection of Renaissance paintings. Her eyes settled on the Mona Lisa in the middle of the wall. Knowing the original was on display in the Louvre, she couldn't help but notice that it certainly made for an excellent replica.

"Gabriel, which painting?" she whispered.

"There's not supposed to be that many on the wall," he replied with angst in his voice as he took in the view through Sam's button camera.

"Well, I just counted twelve, Duval. Which one is it?" Sam responded irritated.

"How should I know? Pick one."

"That's your answer to everything tonight, isn't it?" Sam snapped back.

"How big is the vault, Gabriel?" Alex intervened sensing the two were at loggerheads again.

"As far as I know the size of a shoebox."

By now Alex had pushed her cheek flush against the wall next to one of the paintings and continued along the wall as far as her eyes allowed her to see.

"Don't!" She stopped Sam from lifting one of them away from the wall. "It could have a tripwire."

"You mean like this one?" Sam pointed to a painting of a young boy holding a sword and a shield. Above his head was a halo and large green angel wings extended from his back. His one foot pinned a demon-like creature to the ground while several similar creatures encircled him.

"Any idea what we're dealing with here?" Sam continued.

"The search engine says it's called *Saint Michael Overwhelming the Demon*, painted by Raphael in 1505," Gabriel responded proudly.

"I was talking about the tripwire, Duval."

"Oh yes, of course, what color is it?"

"Black and it's attached to some type of flatpack between the painting and the wall."

Alex and Sam waited while Gabriel researched the alarm system.

"It's a standard sensor pack. The unit operates by monitoring changes in the pressure between the painting and the supporting wall, down to approximately half an ounce. Removal of the painting will release the pressure and activate the alarm. Likewise, the unit will also detect increases in pressure."

"Bottom line, please, Duval. Can we cut the wires?"

"Hold on."

"No! Don't cut the wires. I repeat, don't—"

"We heard you, Gabriel, just tell us what to look for? There has to be a switch or something, right?"

"Affirmative, Alex, it could be via remote control or a release button."

Alex went back to the desk and yanked open the two small

drawers on each side. Seeing nothing that would resemble a switch, she moved across the floor to the bookshelf and skimmed her eyes along the shelves. Still, the result was the same. Pausing next to the desk she decided to move the chair away from the desk and hunched down to see underneath it. Her eyes rested on a silver gun strapped to the table and next to it, a small remote with a red button.

"Think I found it. Ready?" she asked Sam who still stood with his cheek against the wall next to the painting.

"Ready."

She triggered the switch, and Sam heard the faintest sounds of a surging break behind the painting.

"Yep, that did the trick," he commented as he lifted the painting from the wall.

Anticipating a shoebox-sized vault, they instead found one about twice the size in the wall.

"Code please, Duval."

Sam's fingers lingered an inch away from the digital display panel on the vault. The slightest of tremblings was visible in his fingers as he waited for Gabriel to respond.

"Today please, Duval," he urged.

"Copy that. Bravo, three, zero, four, lima, victor, five seven, whiskey, nine."

Surprised the code still worked, the vault opened to reveal a thick antique leather-bound book. Alex pulled the book from the vault. Hand-stitched in brown leather, the book emitted an air of prestige. Gold gilt detail on the spine and a tooled leather cover confirmed it to be dating back to at least the nineteenth to the early twentieth century. Heavier than it looked, she slipped it into her backpack.

"You did it! You got the names!" Gabriel's voice blared into their ears. "Sam, Alex, get out of there. Time to bring these traitors down."

But neither of his two team members answered back.

"Guys, do you copy? You did it, let's get you out of there."

Panic rushed through Gabriel's insides when he repeated his plea and still no answers from either Sam or Alex returned. Seconds later, the speaker system in Francois' basement headquarters delivered the piercing sound that all comms with Alex and Sam had ceased.

A lex blinked several times but still was unable to see anything. She lifted her head and felt the sharp sting on her skull at the back of her head. Everything was dark—too dark to see beyond a foot or two in front of her. Her body was cold as ice, and a foul stench of rat urine lay thick in the air. Her body felt heavy. She attempted to move her hair away from her face but found she couldn't. She tried again realizing her arms were pinned to her sides. Was she lying down on her back? She couldn't tell. It didn't feel like she was sitting either. She tried moving her legs and experienced the same pinned down sensation. She looked down, vaguely seeing the floor beneath her feet. There was something against her back, but she couldn't tell what. She pushed her head back gently and felt a hard column-like surface. Determining it to be a post, she tried wriggling her body free with unsuccessful results. There was no wriggle-room at all.

"Sam? Are you here?" she called out with a dry mouth, but he didn't answer.

"Is anyone here? Hello?"

Still, no sounds came back, aside from squeaking rats somewhere behind her. Bending her hands backward, she stretched her fingers out until she felt Sam's cold hands. She tugged one of his fingers.

"Sam! Wake up. Sam!"

Sam groaned.

"Sam, it's me, wake up. Are you okay?"

"What happened?"

"I'm not sure. Can you move?"

She felt motion behind her as he attempted to move his body.

"No, what's happening? Where are we?"

"I don't know. We have a post or something between us. I think we're tied to it."

"My head hurts," Sam reported.

"Mine too. They must have caught us in the office and hit us with something. I can't remember much."

"Probably have mild concussions."

"Can you see anything from where you are?"

Sam moved his head around and noticed a small window in front of him. "I can see the stars. How romantic?"

"So there's a window?"

"Yep."

"Can we climb through it?"

"You might, but I won't get more than my head through it. There has to be a door here somewhere."

"It's too dark. We need to get out of these ropes, I can't feel my feet anymore," Alex said through chattering teeth, her fingers still clenched around two of Sam's.

"How did they even know we were there? We were so careful with the alarm. Gabriel!" Alex suddenly remembered their hidden mics.

"Gabriel, do you copy?"

Neither heard anything, so she repeated it. Still, Gabriel didn't respond.

"We might have lost the earpieces, Alex, or we're beyond range."

"What about your suit? Are you still wearing your jacket with the camera?"

Sam pushed his chin onto his chest. "I am. I can't see much of anything, but I think all the buttons are still there."

"Good, maybe we're in luck then. Let's try to pull away from each other. We might be able to stretch or loosen the ropes enough for me to wriggle out from underneath it."

Several hours later, after having exhausted themselves in an attempt to free their bodies, they gave up. Alex's body shivered beyond her control, and Sam had tried everything to keep her from passing out.

"Stay with me, Alex, we have a wedding to get to, remember?"

Alex let out a faint moan.

"It will be morning soon, we can't sit under the stars forever. Just hang in there, sweetheart."

Sam was right. It wasn't long after that the sun's light beamed in through the tiny window. Sam had managed to keep Alex awake even though there was more than one occasion he almost fell asleep too.

"Tell me what you see, Alex? Is there a door?"

"What good will that do? We can't get to the door."

"You're not one to quit, Alex. We need to fight our way out of this, just like we have in the past. You're a Hunt and Hunts don't stop fighting back. You hear me?"

Alex lifted her head, turning to take in their surroundings. "I see the door. It's wood with steel reinforcements diagonally across it."

"There's my girl. What else?"

"It looks like we're in a prison cell inside a castle or something. We can't be underground because you saw the stars and now the sunlight."

"Precisely, we're above ground, that's good. I see rats, so there has to be a way in somewhere." Sam dropped his head back and sideways next to the wooden beam that ran up into the roof. It was vaulted resembling that of a small tower. He followed the trusses as far back as his eyes would allow and saw it running in the direction of the door.

"Can you see where the beams lead to?"

"Above the door."

"That's our way out, my love. Can you reach anything that might help us break these ropes?"

Alex turned, searching the wooden post behind her and settled on a rusted nail a few inches above her wrist.

"I think I found something. There's a nail, but I can't reach it."

Sam twisted his head to the side and saw it too. His fingers curled around it, enough for him to push it back and forth several times. Grateful that the wood had weakened over the years it wasn't long before he yanked the nail from the post. He started sawing away at the rope above Alex's wrist. Slowly the rope gave way, and one by one, the strands broke enough for her to free her hand. She wriggled her body, aided by Sam until she was able to slide out from under the ropes. Her limbs were stiff, impacting her mobility to move quickly. Her near-frozen fingers fumbled clumsily with the knots of Sam's ropes until he too was freed.

CHAPTER TWENTY-ONE

As Sam's ropes fell to the floor, chains rattled against the door. Moments later, a key in the lock turned, and the door to their prison cell swung open. Caught off guard, Alex and Sam set eyes on a tall slightly hunched male figure wearing a black executioner's mask. A second, marginally shorter man without a mask, rapidly entered behind him followed by a third, also unmasked. Alex and Sam stared down the barrels of their automatic firearms. Still trying to warm up her stiff limbs, Alex prepared to attack, but she knew this was one fight neither her nor Sam would win in the condition they were in. One of the men grabbed Alex by the arm, pointing the gun firmly to her head while the second unmasked man aimed his weapon at Sam. Without speaking, they ushered the pair toward the door.

"Where are we going?" Alex asked. Still, no one spoke.

The gun jammed into her ribcage, and she continued walking down the corridor away from the cell. Behind her, Sam was forced to follow. Absorbing their surroundings, they both realized they were inside a fortress of some sort. When they slowed down, the men poked the guns harder into their backs.

"Where are you taking us?" Alex tried again. This time the man's hands took hold of her hair, yanking it back hard. Alex reached back in a reflex motion but was shoved hard toward a room leading off from the corridor.

"Stop, you're hurting her!" Sam yelled, for which he received a hard knock in the nape of his neck before being pushed inside the same small room. The unmasked men blindfolded them and tied their hands behind their backs. Forced into chairs on opposite ends of the narrow room, Alex and Sam heard a male voice in the doorway.

"I thought I told you not to meddle in my business?"

Alex instantly recognized his voice. It was the man from her apartment.

"I don't know what you mean," she chanced.

"Oh, I think you do, Miss Hunt. You stuck your nose where it didn't belong. You should have followed my advice and stayed out of it. Now I'm forced to take extreme measures."

The man fell silent for a brief moment before he spoke again.

"Where's the heart and the letter?"

Alex felt a sudden coldness hit her core. Dare she pretend not to know what he was talking about? She didn't answer.

"Miss Hunt, I believe you've been planning a wedding to Dr. Quinn over here. I'm sure you still want that wedding, yes? So I'm going to ask you again, where have you hidden the heart and the letter?"

Alex's shoulders tightened as her entire body went rigid with fear.

"I don't have it anymore."

"That I know, my dear Alex, since I searched your backpack and found my dossier. That only means one thing, you hid the heart somewhere. And since you're not forthcoming, you leave me no choice."

Alex stiffened, unable to speak. Moments later, Sam's painful cries filled the room.

"Stop! Leave him alone!" she yelled, unable to see what they were doing to him. Sam's agonizing cries stopped and turned to heavy panting.

"Leave him alone. I'll give you the heart, but you need to let him go."

"Now, why would I do that? What if you're lying to me, sending me on a wild goose chase? I need him. So, where is the heart?"

"It's in d'Andigné's office, under the rug in the floorboards," she said, instantly loathing herself for being forced to give up their only trump card so quickly.

The men secured both Alex and Sam's feet to the legs of their chairs and weaved the rope through the knots around their wrists. When they were done, she heard the men turn before the door closed and locked behind them. Alex and Sam sat in silence, making sure they had been left alone. She turned her head toward Sam, trying to see from underneath her blindfold.

"Sam?" She whispered. "Are you okay?"

"I'll live. They broke my finger."

Frustrated, Alex pushed her shoulder against her temples in an attempt to remove the blindfold. She managed to move it just enough to see Sam with his head bowed in his chair. They were alone.

"We need to get out of here, Sam, before they come back. They will have no reason to keep us alive any longer once they have the heart back. Can you get up and place the back of your chair against mine? You need to turn to your left."

Sam shuffled his chair around mirrored by Alex on hers. She bumped his broken finger by accident, causing him to cringe with pain.

There was no time for apologies as adrenaline rushed

through her veins. Her fingers fumbled with the tight knots around Sam's wrists. The roughness of the ropes chaffed against her fingertips until she felt the stickiness of fresh blood between her fingers. Desperate for their escape, she was numbed against the pain. One final knot freed Sam's injured hand, sending new spasms of pain through his arm. With his hand untied, using his palm, he pushed his blindfold off his face to restore his sight. Unable to use his broken index finger, he fumbled his way through the knots around his feet while Alex kept going at the knots around his other hand. It took longer than they had hoped for, but their attempt was successful. With Sam mobile, he turned to Alex, pulling her blindfold off first before following through with the rest of her restraints.

With Alex free and looking for a way out, Sam turned his attention to his injury. He forced the broken bone back into place and, using his blindfold, bound his readjusted digit to his third and fourth fingers. The procedure left him breathless with agony.

Alex had already concluded that the door was bolted from the outside, which left only the window as their escape point. In contrast to the much smaller one in their first cell, this one was a large arched window with stained glass. She picked up the chair and threw it through the window. With Sam's help, they used the rope and tied it to one of the iron bars that spanned the width of the window frame. It was hard to determine precisely how high they were, but they estimated it only to be only two stories up. At most, the rope would allow for them to reach the small balcony a bit further down. It would have to suffice.

"You go first," Sam directed.

It took less than twenty seconds for Alex to rappel down to the balcony below, soon followed by Sam. They'd have to take a chance escaping through the building since the rope was too short to deposit them all the way to the ground. The balcony led off a spacious room with an enormous wooden table and chairs set in the middle of the room. The walls were adorned with several paintings similar to the collection seen in the secret fraternity's office.

"This looks like it might be a boardroom," Alex whispered, to which Sam nodded in reply, his attention already occupied by the interconnecting office to the right. The similarities to the other office were undeniable.

"Are you thinking what I'm thinking?" Sam whispered as they entered the adjoining office and laid eyes on the computer standing on the nearby desk.

"I say we check it out. Feels like we might have stumbled onto something," Sam said.

Alex didn't hesitate, and her hands moved the mouse track over the screen. The duo stared at a large logo of a chessboard. In the center of the board, a three-dimensional image of a brass queen chess piece zoomed in and out. The cursor blinked on the screen, waiting for the password to be entered. Alex's fingers hovered over the keys. "Any ideas," she asked Sam.

"Yep just one." Sam held Gabriel's spy tech flash drive between his fingers.

She smiled. "Who would have thought we'd use this?"

She inserted the flash drive into the PC's USB port and watched as the little red light activated the process. Within seconds the blimp on the screen was replaced by a row of fast-moving dots before the computer kicked into a series of flashing screens. Flipping through a sequence of opening files the drive searched through the computer's content before copying the entire contents onto the drive.

"We hit the jackpot, Sam. It's everything. The digital dossier of members' names, activities, algorithms, everything! Who knows how far this dates back and who's all involved?"

"That's great Alex, but I wish this gadget would hurry it along so we can get out of here. I'd hate to lose another finger."

Another fifteen seconds went by. Sam had walked over to the window in an attempt to assess their position.

"You'll never guess where we are, Alex. We're at Versailles. No wonder our comms were out of range. This must be where they operate from."

Just then the flash drive's light switched to green before the computer shut down. Alex snatched the drive from the port. "Done, let's get out of here!"

"Better keep that thing safe, I'm not doing this again." But Sam's words were hardly spoken when Alex reached over and fumbled with his belt buckle.

"Okay, I can't believe I'm going to say this but now isn't the time, Alex."

"Stand still, Sam, you're only making this more difficult."

Confusion mixed with a dash of exhilaration flooded Sam's body all at once as he watched Alex fiddle with the silver clasp in his waist. It was only when the top flipped open to reveal a hidden cavity underneath, that Sam realized what his fiancée was up to. There, neatly tucked around the black leather at his waist was a secret casing in which she hid the flash drive. When she clipped the lid closed and got to her feet, she pecked him on his cheek.

"Oh, you sneaky little minx. You might regret that one of these days. Are you ready to get out of here now?"

"Thought you'd never ask. Lead the way."

To their relief, the building was entirely unoccupied aiding in a clean escape through the front door. Unarmed and with newfound hope the couple ran through the country gardens in the direction of the palace. Dense shrubs and fishponds shouldered the narrow, winding, pebbled path and it dawned on them that the building behind them was the Petit Trianon, Marie Antoinette's private escape. The brown pebbles crunched beneath their feet as they sprinted through the once cherished lavish French gardens of the former Queen. When the palace grounds drew nearer, and they were just about out of danger, the first bullet hit the ground next to them. Unprepared for the sudden attack, they took shelter behind a nearby marble statue. Another rapid succession of shots announced their position had been compromised and they ran toward the shelter of a nearby peristyle. With only a few pillars to shield behind, they were fast running out of options. Surrounded by a canal, the over-running bridge to their right was their only way out. The piercing sound of bullets hitting the marble floor of the veranda forced them toward the bridge. Suddenly aware of the multitude of footsteps fast approaching them from all angles, they knew they were outnumbered. Unable to fight back, trapped between an onslaught of angry mobsters, Alex and Sam surrendered.

CHAPTER TWENTY-TWO

Led by a team of seven armed men, Alex and Sam reluctantly walked toward their vehicle. Vulnerable and physically dehydrated from the past night's torturous events they had little resilience to fight the men. Again their hands were bound and their eyes covered before the men shoved them into the vehicle's trunk. The defeated pair lay silently waiting for the car to drive off.

"Sam, this might be the end."

"Don't say that, sweetheart. We'll find a way to escape."

Alex paused, and with deep sadness, she whispered, "If we don't, know that I've always loved you. You saved me from myself. That day on the plane, when we first met on the way to Tanzania, I knew we were meant to be together. Perhaps you were right, and I should have taken that desk job instead."

"We're going to get out of this, Alex! We've been through this and worse over all the years we've been together. We're a strong team and we'll think of something. You're the smartest person I know. We're going to get out of this." Sam's stern voice did little to console or encourage Alex at this point. From behind her blindfold, she heard him wrestle in an attempt to free his hands.

"Can you use your mouth to pull the blindfold off my eyes?" Sam urged, but she didn't react.

"Alex, stay focused! We can do this. Use your mouth and get my blindfold off."

They lay facing each other, so when Alex still didn't respond, Sam leaned in and caught her blindfold between his teeth. The grip was enough to lower the blindfold around her neck, urging her to reciprocate, which she did.

Seeing Sam's eyes filled her with strength as it so often did and when he instructed her to turn her back to his and their fingers started at the knots, her fear all but subsided.

But, much to their dismay, their efforts were fruitless when the vehicle stopped before any of the knots were untied. With the trunk open and their blindfolds off, they caught sight of the man wearing the black executioner's mask. The armed men hastily replaced their blindfolds and dragged Alex and Sam from the car. Dread and fear raged through their bodies, knowing full well an executioner symbolized death. Alex stumbled to the ground when one of the men shoved her forward.

"What do you want from us?" Sam shouted. "We gave you what you wanted, now let us go."

The men ignored them, pushing and shoving them to keep walking. When they finally stopped, they were forced to their knees. Exposed and terrified, Alex and Sam waited for their fateful death. When, after what seemed like an eternity of tortured silence, no shots were fired, Sam pleaded again.

"Let her go and take me. I was the one who infiltrated your secret meeting. She had nothing to do with it. D'Andigné contacted me. Leave her out of this."

Stunned, Alex choked on the lump that sat wedged in her throat and prevented her from speaking. Sam didn't deserve to die. It was all her fault.

Unexpectedly their blindfolds were yanked off their faces and, for the first time, Alex and Sam got a grasp on what their futures held. Directly in front of them, as they knelt in its shadow, was a larger than life guillotine. Next to it, the executioner stood waiting. Terror ripped through their loins settling in the pit of their stomachs as reality washed over them. Aware of the gunman at the rear of them, the silence finally broke with an unidentified tapping and footsteps behind them.

"I thought you might appreciate dying like this since this is what brought you here in the first place." The voice behind them was now all too familiar.

"You got what you wanted, now let us go," Alex pleaded.

"Now don't go spoiling our fun, Alex. You know, back during the Revolution this was how they entertained the crowds. Petty thieves like you received their punishment in this exact spot. That glistening silver blade over there has made many heads roll, and today, the honor falls on you."

"You're a coward whoever you are. Why don't you show your face instead of hiding behind us?" Sam taunted him.

The challenge worked, and they heard the man's footsteps, mingled with the peculiar clicking noise from before, approach and stop before them. Sam gasped as the man came into full view and his eyes settled on the recognized pewter cane he'd first seen back at the police station in London.

"You! You're the Queen?"

"You know him?" Alex gasped, surprised that Sam knew the man who was responsible for her attack in her apartment.

"He's the guy from the police station. The one who was behind my interrogation."

"Well done, Sam, I knew you'd remember my face."

"I never forget the face of a traitor. You won't get away with this. I don't care how much power you think you have."

"Oh, I already have, Sam. You see, The Resistance is much bigger than the two of you might think. We're a family; entrenched in governments, financial sectors, law societies, you name it. We own the world. There isn't a country on the globe we don't own, and we've been doing it for centuries."

"You're criminals fighting against justice," Alex injected.

"Justice! We are justice, Alex. That's what The Resistance is: *Liberté, égalité, fraternité.* We resist being ruled over."

"So your secret brotherhood killed an innocent child, royalty, only to rule your own order."

"The dauphin was what we call collateral damage, Alex. Besides, we never killed the boy. We just made the world believe that we did."

"Nice try. We saw the heart and the doctor's confession remember."

"Oh, the doctor, he was nothing but a quack, a pawn in the greater plan, conned into thinking he did the autopsy on the real dauphin. The heart belonged to the young boy's brother who died of natural causes two years before he was taken. See, even mother nature had a hand in this."

"What happened to the boy if he lived? He had the right to take a throne that was destined for him."

"The boy and his delightful sister were adopted and lived a long, healthy life, and we took care of France and the rest of the world. And as for my dear friend Maurice, we had to kill him. He knew too much. The stupid man took it upon himself to have DNA tests done on the heart and traced it to a royal descendant in Normandy. We couldn't let that happen. But who knew the man would involve you? D'Andigné always did think he was smarter than me."

Alex fought against the anger that threatened to overwhelm her.

"Now, which one of you wants to go first, huh? I have a meeting to get to, so let's get on with business, shall we? How about we show some chivalry and allow the lady to go first? Think you can watch your fiancée's head roll?"

Alex and Sam were numb with fear and disgust. The man with the cane stopped talking and nodded to his men to take Alex to the guillotine.

"You don't have to do this! Let her go!" Sam shouted in anguish, tears streaming down his face, but they ignored his desperate plea. Unable to look away, he watched Alex climb the wooden steps to where she met the hooded executioner. When they forced Alex to her knees in front of the guillotine and left her alone in the hands of the executioner, the fear inside her gave way to serenity.

"Don't say a word and do exactly as I tell you," the executioner whispered next to her. A surge of adrenaline engulfed her when she recognized his voice. He pulled her to her feet and proceeded with a dramatic display by which he delivered her sentence, all the while, discreetly slicing a blade between her bound wrists. After reciting another sequence of dramatic words, he slipped a gun into her hand.

Sam, filled with disgust, listened as his fiancée's judgment was spoken over her. Consumed by guilt and hatred, he stared into her eyes. But instead of defeat, her eyes revealed the opposite. Confusion ripped through his torture when Alex's eyes suddenly declared victory. At that moment, he found himself yielding to what had always been their secret weapon—communication without words. Sam wiped his face on his shoulder and honed in on his fiancée's face. And what followed next, neither could have ever anticipated.

When the executioner spoke again, he delivered his final sentence—Victory, equality, liberty and ripped his hood from his head. Seconds after his signal, an onslaught of special forces descended upon the small gathering.

S till shaken by the dramatic and unexpected turn of events, Alex faced Count Etiénne du Bois.

"You saved our lives, thank you."

"I wish I could take all the credit but I can't. Meet the brain behind the operation." Etiénne pointed his chin out to where Chief Inspector Shawn McDowell stepped out of a police vehicle.

"You? You're the brain behind this?" Sam asked, astonished.

"He's been on it for nearly two decades," Etiénne said proudly. "Meet Mr. Anonymous. He was dealt his lot when his father passed down his inheritance. He comes from a long lineage of Resistance members, but the man has a good heart and decided to infiltrate the movement. I've been working undercover for him since we first met ten years ago."

"I couldn't have done it without you, my friend," McDowell declared. "In fact, the entire team went above and beyond on this one."

One more police car pulled up behind them and a still stunned Alex and Sam watched with disbelief as Francois and Gabriel approached them.

"Well, what do you know?" Sam commented. "You pulled the wool over my eyes, Duval."

"Sorry, Sam, duty called."

"I guess it will be a good time then to return this." Sam retrieved the flash drive from his buckle and dropped it into Gabriel's hand.

The ALEX HUNT Adventures continue in The BARI BONES. Available in eBook and Paperback **(https://books2read.com/TheBariBones)**

The world knows him as Santa Claus or Father Christmas, but his official name has been Saint Nicholas of Myra for over seventeen hundred years, and someone will kill over one gift he's left behind.

When Alex and Sam take a vacation on board a chartered yacht in the Adriatic, their tranquil escape comes to a grinding halt. In the wrong place at the wrong time, they are drawn into a world of biochemical warfare threatening to destroy countless innocent lives.

What lurks at the center of it all are the remains of a seventeen-hundred-year-old Christian saint whose bones secrete a liquid believed to possess immense healing powers. For centuries the Roman Catholic Church in Italy has kept the elixir sacred; extracted only once a year to heal the sick. However, things go dreadfully wrong, and the revered fluid goes missing.

Now, relying on their unique skills and valor to take on a powerful enemy, Alex and Sam are in a race against time to find the essence and prevent it from landing in the wrong hands. Will they have what is necessary to stop a ruthless enemy before millions of innocent people die?

Join them in another riveting adventure as they travel

between China, Greece, and Italy in a quest to save the world!

The Bari Bones is Book 5 in the action-packed Alex Hunt Adventure Thriller series.

Inspired by true historical facts and events. Also suitable as a standalone novel.

*Includes Bonus content and a free digital copy of the series prequel.

Receive a FREE copy of the prequel and see where it all started!

NOT AVAILABLE ANYWHERE ELSE!

Click on image or enter http://download.urcelia.com in your browser

MORE BOOKS BY URCELIA TEIXEIRA

ALEX HUNT Adventure Thrillers

Also suited as standalone novels

The PAPUA INCIDENT - Prequel (sign up to get it FREE)

The RHAPTA KEY

The GILDED TREASON

The ALPHA STRAIN

The DAUPHIN DECEPTION

The BARI BONES

The CAIAPHAS CODE

FREE BONUS - BEHIND THE BOOK

The Young Dauphin

Upon researching this book I came across so many fantastic articles, photos and facts. While there was a LOT of research done, I thought to share just a few of the facts and images that I know would complement the story.

Download the **EXCLUSIVE** condensed copy of my research file here Behind The Dauphin Deception (http://bit.ly/Behind-the-dauphin-deception)

If you enjoyed this book, I would sincerely appreciate it if you could take the time to **leave a review**. It would mean so much to me!

For sneak previews, free books and more,

Join my mailing list

No-Spam Newsletter
ELITE SQUAD

FOLLOW Urcelia Teixeira

BookBub has a New Release Alert. Not only can you check out the latest deals, but you can also get an email when I release my next book by following me here

https://www.bookbub.com/authors/urcelia-teixeira

Website:
https://www.urcelia.com

Facebook:
https://www.facebook.com/urceliabooks

Twitter:
https//www.twitter.com/UrceliaTeixeira

ABOUT THE AUTHOR

Urcelia Teixeira is an author of fast-paced archaeological action-adventure novels with a Christian nuance.

Her Alex Hunt Adventure Thriller Series has been described by readers as 'Indiana Jones meets Lara Croft with a twist of Bourne'. She read her first book when she was four and wrote her first poem when she was seven. And though she lived vicariously through books, and her far too few travels, life happened. She married the man of her dreams and birthed three boys (and added two dogs, a cat, three chickens, and some goldfish!) So, life became all about settling down and providing a means to an end. She climbed the corporate ladder, exercised her entrepreneurial flair and made her mark in real estate.

Traveling and exploring the world made space for child-friendly annual family holidays by the sea. The ones where she succumbed to building sandcastles and barely got past reading the first five pages of a book. And on the odd occasion she managed to read fast enough to page eight, she was confronted with a moral dilemma as the umpteenth expletive forced its way off just about every page!

But by divine intervention, upon her return from yet another male-dominated camping trip, when fifty knocked hard and fast on her door, and she could no longer stomach the profanities in her reading material, she drew a line in the sand and bravely set off to create a new adventure!

It was in the dark, quiet whispers of the night, well past midnight late in the year 2017, that Alex Hunt was born.

Her philosophy

From her pen flow action-packed adventures for the armchair traveler who enjoys a thrilling escape. Devoid of the usual profanity and obscenities, she incorporates real-life historical relics and mysteries from exciting places all over the world. She aims to kidnap her reader from the mundane and plunge them into feel-good riddle-solving quests filled with danger, sabotage, and mystery!

For more visit www.urcelia.com or email her on books@urcelia.com

facebook.com/urceliateixeira

twitter.com/urcelia_teixeira

instagram.com/urceliateixeira

COPYRIGHT © 2019 BY URCELIA TEIXEIRA

Paperback © ISBN: 978-0-6399665-9-5

Independently Published by Urcelia Teixeira

www.urcelia.com

books@urcelia.com

Made in the USA
Las Vegas, NV
01 March 2021

18816478R00163